ASSASSIN'S CHOICE

MONIQUE SINGLETON

USA TODAY AND INTERNATIONAL BESTSELLING AUTHOR

VINCI
BOOKS

ASSASSIN'S CHOICE

MONIQUE SINGLETON

vinci
BOOKS

Years ago, I allowed myself to entertain the idea of maybe, just maybe, writing a book.

Publishing was not part of the equation then. Just the writing was a big enough step.

The first book was written, and a second followed. Then another. I kept on writing. And now this book before you, is the sixth I've have published.

I don't do this alone. I couldn't.

There is a team of great people helping me, from my loving family and friends—who support me, whatever harebrained idea I think of next— to Richard Butler my editor, to all of you fantastic readers who have made my dream come true.

Thank you from the bottom of my heart.

Vinci Books

vinci-books.com

Published by Vinci Books Ltd in 2026

1

A CIP catalogue record for this book is available from the British Library.
Paperback ISBN: 9781036701550

The EU GPSR authorised representative is Logos Europe, 9 rue Nicolas
Poussion, 17000 La Rochelle, France
contact@logoseurope.eu

Chapter One

So that's my target.

Nice.

Shame I have to kill him.

But who says I can't have some fun first?

I watched the ash-blonde man on the tennis court from behind my designer sunglasses. His white T-shirt clung to his sculptured body like a second skin. The sweaty wet patches showed his coffee-coloured skin under the thin almost translucent material. His shorts strained at the thighs with the swelling of the thick muscles as he ran forward, his racket hitting the ball over the net at the last possible moment. He stood up to his full height and wiped his face with the underside of his shirt, offering everyone who was watching—and there were a lot—a great view of his six-pack. I got a fantastic glimpse of his tight buttocks under the clay-stained shorts as he turned to walk back to the line. Very nice.

Back in place, he bent his knees and leant forward, his arms tense as he waited for the next volley.

I could watch him all day.

This was Metisse. A playboy millionaire who spent his fun time excelling in all kinds of sports. His family was old money, with origins going back as far as the eighteenth century. At six feet, two hundred pounds he was a big man, athletic and easy to smile. The coffee-brown of his skin colour spoke of mixed racial heritage. His hair—dyed almost white—formed a stark contrast to the darkness of his skin and his eyes. All in all, he was a tasty mix of everything I like.

He was also a Sabretooth shapeshifter, the leader of the local clan. And according to our research, he was one of the two main players in the war to come. That made him my business.

The game continued for another half hour.

I thoroughly enjoyed every minute of my surveillance. My body was getting almost as hot as he looked, and it had nothing to do with the nice sunny weather.

There was a collective sigh of admiration on the tennis club terrace when he pulled the soaked shirt up over his head. The material had hinted at a fantastic physique and no one was disappointed. There were giggles from the only two guys at the terrace tables, all the other seats were taken by women. This guy was a magnet.

A tall blonde Playboy-bunny of about twenty-one skittled over the tennis court towards the white-haired hunk and threw her arms around his broad shoulders. His right arm snaked around her small waist as he kissed her. Disappointed women all around me drank the remnants of their wine and stood up, ready to get back to their regular and boring lives with their less-than-perfect but very rich husbands. All would dream well tonight. I stayed where I was.

I wasn't here for a dream.

The blonde bimbo giggled all the way up to the terrace. Metisse pulled back a chair for her and glanced my way. Our eyes locked. He cocked his head slightly in acknowledgement of a connection we both felt. My lips curled up in a smile as I pushed the sunglasses back over my now yellow-hued eyes.

Ten minutes later I signalled the waiter for the bill, gave him my platinum card and stood up to put on my light, summer coat. The waiter returned my card and with one last smile at Metisse, I turned and left the tennis club. He would see me again, only I would determine when.

The game has started.

Chapter Two

It probably wouldn't be a stretch to say that I like to live dangerously.

Life gets to be quite boring when you're immortal. Been there, done that, becomes; been there, and there, and there. You get my drift. Even the most exciting adventures start to go stale after you've done them four times.

Eternity seems like such a good idea. It is on the surface, but once you get down to the nitty-gritty; it's just plain boring. And boredom breeds mischievousness. At least it does with me. And when I get naughty, sparks start to fly.

I've never been a good girl. How does the saying go? "Good girls go to heaven; bad girls go wherever they want." Well, heaven is out of the question for me, so I might as well have a lot of fun here.

My kind of fun, along with my job, brought me here; to the "paranormal-central" in the US. This has got to be the one place in the States, probably even in the whole world, where you can find just about every kind of paranormal creature not known to man. If, that is, you know where to look, and what to look for.

Me, I know exactly what I'm looking for. And this mission was starting to be a lot more pleasurable than I'd anticipated. I've had much worse. Definitely ones that weren't as easy on the eyes.

This was at least an interesting assignment, and it offered me ample opportunity to have some fun on the way. I guess there was a deadline, but I'm not very good with those anyway. I do things my way. And fuck them if they didn't like that.

"Them" was the Council. The entity that ruled the paranormal world; the world that lived on earth, unbeknownst to all the humans who also inhabit this planet. They stuck me with this mission. I still think it was a way for them to get back at me for all the grief I've given them. Funny really how what looks like a bum job can turn out to be so satisfying after all. I don't think they had this in mind when they gave me the assignment.

I know they didn't expect the end result.

Let's backtrack a bit.

Chapter Three

I hated the pompousness of the whole place. It was so cliché. Completely over the top. From the three-story-high ceiling with all the ornate columns that lined the side of the great hall, to the gilded paintings of heroes from times gone by. It was just too much. The heavy drapes over the three-metre-high windows felt stuffy and hardly let in any light. The musky smell was barely camouflaged by incense and bright blue cold fires. The presence of supernatural energy —or magic as humans call it—was evident in the moving statues, the tingle in the air and the hairs that stood up on the back of my neck.

This was the Council's home ground. All of it designed to impress. It did most of the time, only not with me. I don't impress easily. Especially not with ostentatious stage-setting. That's how I looked at it, a stage. A story. Not real.

Even with my usually quiet supple-leather boots there was an echo as I made my way down the centre of the enormous hall to the horseshoe table set on a platform under the glass skylight. The colours in the glass shone strange hues down on the congregation sitting in the stiff high-backed chairs on the opposite side of the table. They were all facing the hall. Facing me.

As I neared the platform it became clear that almost all of the council members were in attendance.

Wow! Since when did I merit that kind of attention?

I didn't. And I didn't want it either. Hmmm. Not a good sign. I stepped up on to the platform as was expected and moved forward until I was level with the two ends of the horseshoe.

To my left three seats were taken by members of different creature's clans. There is no other way of describing them. Two vampires, a man and a woman, and a shapeshifter currently blue and covered in scales; must be a fashion thing I'm not familiar with. The Vampires were as always stiff and unmoving. Dressed from head to toe in gothic black and dark red velvet, they looked like they'd stepped out of a really bad horror movie. So stereotypical. No creativity or imagination there. The shapeshifter—I couldn't tell if it was male or female—was at least colourful.

To my right the occupants of the seats were more human looking. That didn't mean anything. Just that they had chosen a more mortal visage. For now.

My attention was drawn to the person in the centre of the horseshoe. Standing ten feet tall when on his feet, Cantix still towered over everyone else while seated in the biggest chair at the table. He was as wide in the shoulders as a bull and his face showed the same characteristics. Officially a mage, this man had many more talents than just magic. He was the supreme ruler of the Council. Formally a democracy, no one on the Council, or in the supernatural world for that matter, doubted who actually ran the show.

To the right of Cantix's chair stood a regal woman. The

look on her face was cold, icy. Enough to send most people running. Her dark, green-black gown hugged her straight figure. Frankly she looked like a plank. One with a very bad attitude. The only thing that had any form at all in the whole picture was her hair. The continuous movement of the bright green tresses looked like a mass of snakes. How she did it I don't know. But I was sure that it was a trick of some kind.

This was Aquanaris. The official Oracle to the Council. It was rumoured she and Cantix were having an affair. Well, they definitely deserved each other. Though trying to think of what their sexual escapade would look like stretched even my overactive imagination. Whatever the truth was to the rumours, they were close. That much was clear. Cantix listened to what she said and acted on what he presumed was the truth.

It's an understatement to say that she and I didn't get along. I flatly refused to bow to what I was sure were her lies. There is no such thing as a genuine Oracle. In my opinion they are all frauds. And she was the worst. Cantix and the rest of the Council were of a different opinion and easily led by her rantings. We'd clashed before more than once, with me contradicting all her statements. If she was legit, then I had even more reason to stay as far away from her as possible.

I bowed to Cantix as was expected. He was, after all, my commander-in-chief. Aquanaris merited only a slight nod. This was not lost on Cantix who I'm sure secretly enjoyed our little stabs at each other. The edge of his thin lips curved ever so slightly upwards in what, with a bit of fantasy, could be mistaken for a smile as he glanced at his Oracle.

'Altermichan.' Cantix had a habit of using my full

name. Another thing I disliked about the man. I hate my name. It feels so restricting. Don't know why, it just feels that way.

'Your excellence,' I replied.

'Thank you for coming on such short notice.' Yeah, as if I had a choice. A notice from Cantix wasn't actually a voluntary thing. It was a summons; mandatory. Now get to the point, will you?

'Something has come to my attention, and I need your assistance.'

I nodded. What else was I supposed to do. His requests were not exactly something you could refuse. At least not if you wanted to stay alive.

'Aquanaris has seen a very bleak future.'

So, what's new? I don't think she's ever seen anything that would be remotely positive.

I had to reign in my emotions. Cantix was sending me strange looks.

'There will be a war. One that will expose our kind to the humans. This will violate the first objective and must be avoided at all costs.'

The first objective; never let the human world know that we are here. And by "we" the objective means any supernatural creature. Ours' is a secret world. We are around humans every day but must never let our presence be known. Some have in the past, and that usually didn't end well.

'Therefore, we need to take action.'

Here the "we" meant "you". Whatever it was, it was quickly becoming my problem.

'What was the prophecy?' I aimed my question at Cantix and flatly refused to ask Aquanaris. This would no doubt piss her off—well tough.

Cantix smiled again at my childish antics and turned to his Oracle. 'Please Aquanaris, enlighten us.'

The Oracle stepped forward from behind the throne-like chair and placed an intricately decorated piece of animal skin on the table. At least I hoped it was animal skin. With her, you never knew. There have been rumours.

The monotonous humming and the way she waved her long thin hands over the parchment was hypnotising. My eyes followed her right hand and then transferred to the left as the two met over the middle of the decorations. Small plumes of green-blue smoke wound through her fingers as she continued to move. My ears blocked out any other sounds than that of her voice. I was beginning to feel light-headed. Weak. I shook my head in an attempt to expel the hold I could feel encroaching on my consciousness. No way. No way would I let myself get under her spell.

I stared through the smoke at the skin. The decorations moved, forming pictures, though what precisely was unclear.

Aquanaris clapped her hands loudly, the sound carried and echoed in the vast chamber. I jumped backwards, my right hand grabbing the heft of my sword. My nerves felt frayed by the unexpected sound.

Aquanaris lips were curled up in a vicious smile. This was payback for my earlier slight. I should have known she wouldn't let that one pass in a hurry.

I felt the blush on my cheeks as I stepped forward again to peer into the softly dispersing smoke.

The skin clearly showed a new image. There were two figures on the parchment. One a Werewolf standing on its hind legs, mouth agape leaning forward, its blood-coated fangs reaching for the opponent; a Sabretooth that towered above it. The long canines of the feline were bright red, and the claws ripped into the Wolf's body. As I watched, the image moved, playing out a scene in a movie. The Sabretooth slashed its claws again and again, spraying blood in all directions. The Wolf struggled to stay upright but finally dropped to its knees. One bite of the cat's long canines ripped out the Wolf's throat and the body fell to the floor on top of a multitude of other corpses. The image zoomed out to show a large battlefield strewn with dead Werewolves, Sabres and human-like creatures. It was a massacre.

'This is what will happen,' the Oracle proclaimed. 'The Wolves and the Sabres will fight to the death. They will expose us all and a war with the humans will be inevitable.'

I thought the conclusion was quite a stretch, but I got the drift.

It was bad.

Chapter Four

I willed my eyes to leave the parchment and look into Cantix's face. His shrewd eyes watched my every reaction. The lines on his forehead were deep and pronounced as he contemplated what to say next.

I beat him to it, 'why me?' I asked.

'Because you are the best shapeshifter we have. You can walk amongst both tribes without them noticing. You can assimilate until the time is right to stop all this.'

'By stop all this you mean kill them?' I'm kind of direct. Don't know if he appreciated it. But that wasn't my problem. He knew me.

To the side I heard the Oracle's sharp intake of breath.

Cantix nodded. 'If necessary.' He had a bit more of a sense of humour than his seer. Besides, he knew that I was the one holding the short straw. You don't say "no" to Cantix. Not if you value your life. I think I already mentioned that.

'Yes, you may need to kill the ringleaders. Your mission

is to make sure there are no more thoughts of rebellion and war.'

Rebellion? Now that was a strange choice of words. Rebellion against whom? I decided not to react to what I was sure was a slip of the tongue. I would draw my conclusions later.

'How do I know which ones I have to kill?' I asked. 'The prophecy didn't exactly zoom in on personal characteristics. Not sure I could pick those two out of a crowd.' Why, oh why, did I always have to push the cynical jabs home? Cantix laughed out loud, a deep rumbling sound that reverberated through the hall and shook the platform we were on.

'You will have to find out,' he finally answered. 'Aquanaris will fill you in on the details.'

Oh shit. Not her. I'd have to spend more time with Mrs. Plank.

Cantix pushed his chair backwards and stood to his full height. He towered over me, my head barely reaching the centre of his chest, and I'm not small. My body urged me to step backwards, but I refused to comply. No way would I give in to the intimidation that Cantix was known for.

'I will leave you two to work out the details,' he said as he turned to leave the platform. 'I expect frequent feedback from you Altermichan, and for that I will assign you a mage. Through him you can report back to me.' A mage? Hell no.

'I work alone,' I stated. Frustration clear in my voice.

'Not this time.' He dismissed me as easily as that. With him, the other members of the Council vacated the stage, leaving me alone with Aquanaris who was beaming from ear to ear. She was enjoying this no end. My big mouth and attitude regularly get me into trouble, and this was one of the big ones. I had a major issue with the Oracle. She was curious. Much too curious.

And I had enough to hide.

Aquanaris moved around the table towards the side where I stood. Her tall stiff frame glided over the floor, her long gown swishing across the stone tiles.

She came close—much too close—and I stepped back until my buttocks hit the tabletop, effectively stopping my progress. This was not going well. My hand moved towards my sword. The grip offered me some comfort. Aquanaris' eyes strayed to the weapon. It was legendary, as was my prowess in using it. Her advance faltered and she stopped a metre in front of me.

The air between us tingled. The energy raised the hairs on the back of my neck. I felt the fur pricking through the skin alongside my spine. I had to control it. To let the beast out now would be extremely detrimental to my longevity.

I slowly relaxed my hand and let it fall from the hilt of the sword.

The action wasn't lost on the Oracle. I saw her eyes register it and noticed a slight soothing of her stiff exterior. The minimal rise in her chest indicated she was breathing again. Good to know I had that effect on her. I'd keep that in mind.

'Tell me about the prophecy,' I said, slightly more friendly than I normally would be. I needed to diffuse the situation. Get her away from me. 'The sooner we start, the quicker I can get this whole thing over with.'

She nodded; her eyes tried to lock on to mine. I avoided her. Not sure that she wouldn't see the beast inside. She was clever.

During the next hour she filled me in on what they

knew, which was precious little. A lot of "ifs" and "maybes." Not very concrete. The main gist of the whole thing was what Cantix already told me. I was to find out who the two leaders were and kill them before they started the whole mess.

Chapter Five

Trust Aquanaris to find the geekiest mage ever born.

The guy was tiny; the top of his head only just came up to my chin. His face was chiselled and stark, almost cadaverous. Was there no flesh on this guy? Frankly, I had to sniff the air to make sure I wasn't talking to a dead body. Nope, no death smell, no tell-tale earthy decomposition scent. The guy was alive. His deep-set eyes shifted from one side to the other as he shuffled forward from behind the Oracle. He wouldn't look me in the eye, or her for that matter. His fidgeting was already getting on my nerves.

This was going to be a long mission.

'This is Alex,' Aquanaris introduced us. I nodded. More would probably have terrified him.

'Hullo.' I could just about make out his whispered acknowledgement.

'And what exactly is Alex going to do?' My question was aimed at the Oracle. He wouldn't have answered anyway.

'He will be your liaison with the Council,' she explained. 'Alex will report back to us on your progress.'

Great, just what I needed. The Council looking over my shoulder all the time.

'He will also assist you with research and any other help that you need.'

I looked at the small timid man again. I couldn't fathom what assistance he could offer during an assassination. He'd probably shit his pants at the first sight of blood.

'You sure he'll be able to stomach the kills? And the mopping up of the blood and guts?' I asked, observing his reaction more than the Oracle's this time. I wasn't disappointed. He blanched and his eyes opened in shock. Guess she hadn't told him about that part yet.

'He will surprise you,' she answered.

Yeah, and himself too if he's supposed to keep up with me. I didn't have the patience for this. Nor did I want a tag-along. I resolved to get rid of him at the first possible opportunity.

I turned and started to walk away. About ten steps on, I stopped and turned back. Alex was still in the same place, cowering behind Aquanaris.

'You coming? Or what?' I said impatiently. He was getting on my bad side already.

My comment—with just the right amount of threat in the tone—got through the scared exterior and he scrambled towards me, almost falling off the Council's platform. He flailed his arms but managed to stay upright as he made up the distance.

I sighed, disgusted at the wimp, turned and walked on out of the stupid castle. I'd been here much too long for my comfort. Every time I was around the Council, I needed to call on every fibre of restraint I had within me just to leave them alive. And now they'd stuck me with a new almost impossible mission and saddled me up with a dimwit to boot.

Just my luck.

One comment kept nagging at my brain as I walked back down the endless hall on my way out of the huge building: "Rebellion".

Now what was all that about?

Chapter Six

Away from the Council, Alex started to defrost a bit. His fidgeting continued, but not to the same nervous extent I saw earlier. We were back in the "normal" world in my off-road jeep on a stretch of deserted road in the Appalachian Mountains. The vehicle bumped and bounced over the dirt-road as I drove much too fast. My immortality made me reckless. Not only that, but I wanted to keep the mage on his toes. The sooner he started to really fear me, the easier it would be to get rid of him. There were things the Council was not allowed to know about me, not yet. So, this guy snooping around would not do at all.

He hung on to the doorhandle for dear life, his face almost as pale as earlier. Well, welcome to my life, I thought and laughed internally. The poor schmuck would not have an enjoyable time shadowing me.

The dirt-road made way for an Interstate as we almost launched off the rough terrain into civilisation. A tiny, muffled scream sounded from my left. Again, I smiled.

We continued in silence for almost a hundred miles. At

some point I glanced to my left, almost sure that he had fallen asleep, but no; he was observing me.

'Where are we going?' he asked.

'To where I currently live,' I answered. 'We need to find the targets.' He nodded his agreement. 'Do you have any idea where to start?' I asked.

He thought on that for a few moments. Just before I repeated the question, he replied. 'We know that they are large Werewolf and Sabre communities,' he said thoughtfully. 'They will probably be somewhere near each other, or there wouldn't be a real threat of war.' Hmm, maybe he would be useful after all.

'Do you have a computer?' he asked.

'Yes, of course,' I answered slightly vexed. It hardly registered with him.

'And good Internet connection?'

I nodded. I would humour him for the moment. But he had better show me results. Quickly.

'Good, then I'll get set up as soon as we get there.' He pulled his rucksack out from under the seat and rummaged in the contents. The smell that came out of the bag was surprisingly sweet. I expected his possessions to have a more unwashed and sweaty scent, his extra clothes dank and reeking, not the soft flowery bouquet of laundry softener. He retrieved a small silver coloured tablet, flipped the lid, linked to a mobile hotspot on his iPhone and started to type away feverishly. He wasn't one to linger, that was for sure.

We continued without speaking, the only sound from him was the soft ticking of his fingers on the tablet as he noted his findings.

He might just be a help after all.

Who knew?

Chapter Seven

I don't know what kind of wizard he was, but his prowess on the computer was astounding. I'm not a novice to technology, but he outshone me by miles. Within two hours of our arrival at my temporary home, he had both my computers and his own tablet and laptop searching the dark net. We reasoned that the regular internet wouldn't yield anything worthwhile due to the intrinsic secrecy of the paranormal world. Given enough time, we might have been able to piece together something from indirect information, but we didn't have that luxury. Besides, it would be a waste of time; the dark web would yield what we needed to know.

A ping sounded off Alex's laptop and he instantly rushed to the machine. I sat back and waited. If there was anything worth mentioning, he would inform me.

The guy seemed transformed. This was clearly his domain and he was an expert. Gone was the nervous fidgeting. His eyes no longer flitted from one side to the other. He was deep in concentration, softly speaking his thoughts out loud. If the situation wasn't so serious, I would laugh.

I had to bite my tongue to stop asking what the computer had found.

'Right, right.' His murmurings just made me more curious.

'For fuck's sake.' I couldn't take it anymore. 'What have you found?' This was getting on my nerves.

Alex looked up from the computer screen. His face was flustered, almost as if he was surprised there was someone else in the room. Man, this guy was weird. He'd completely zoned out. Left the world as we know it.

'Uh. Yes.' The words were spoken hesitantly. I cocked my head to the side and raised my eyebrows. Come on Alex, get your act together. 'Yes, yes, um, I have found something.'

'You going to tell me? Or should I beat it out of you?' The tone of my voice registered in the shock on his face. He paled to a decidedly sickly grey. Good, the little shit was still scared of me. Keep that thought.

'There are three places in the world where there are large Werewolf packs and Sabre clans close together. One is in the Ukraine and two are here in the US.'

'We can scratch the one in Europe,' I deduced. 'Aquanaris was resolute it would happen here on American soil.'

'Ok, so that leaves two.' He scrolled through the images again on both of the computers then turned the screens to face me.

'This,' his hand tapped the top of the laptop screen. 'This is in Florida. Just off the Keys. It's an option because there is a very large Wolf pack there. The Sabres are just pushing the boundaries trying to establish a territory of their own. That could be the catalyst to the war.' He didn't sound all that sure of himself.

He moved to the second screen, the one that was

attached to my stationary computer. 'This place is Waisland. It's in the foothills of the Montana Rocky Mountains.'

My mind wandered. Waisland. Yeah, I'd heard of that town. Just about everyone in the paranormal world heard of it at some time. It had the highest number of resident paranormal creatures in the US, debatably even in the world. It was a place my mother had steered us clear of, even though I'd been desperate to go there. "Not yet" was what she repeated every time I begged to go to Waisland. I'd heard and read so much about the place. With so many people living there like me, maybe I would finally fit in. And then, just before she left me, she mentioned the place again.

'… very old.' I heard the last words of Alex's sentence.

'What?' I interrupted him. 'Could you repeat that?'

'From where?'

He was unsure of what I meant. Hadn't I been listening? Well. Yes, I had, up till he mentioned Waisland. My dark features must have answered him, because he started again, somewhat haltingly.

'The other place is Waisland, but I don't think that this is it.'

'Why not?'

'Well…'

'Aren't there Werewolves and Sabres there?'

'Yes, there are,' he stuttered. 'There are really big factions too.'

'But?' I asked menacingly. My eyebrows creased and my eyes were no doubt fierce.

'But…well…they have been there for hundreds of years. Both of the groups. They've had a lasting peace. I…I didn't think that they would really be contenders.'

'Even long-standing peace treaties can be broken,' I answered.

Waisland was calling to me. I'd never been there, not even nearby. Deep in my gut I knew what I was seeking was there. Only thing I didn't know was whether that was the mission, or something completely different.

Alex stayed quiet. He observed me. I would have to watch out with this one. Just when I thought I had him figured out; he turned a leaf. Well, fuck him. And fuck the Council who sent him.

'Find out more about Waisland,' I ordered as I got up from the seat and walked to the exit. I grabbed the keys to my car and opened the door.

'Where are you going?' he asked.

'What's it to you?'

'We're partners.'

'Partners?' The venom in my tone was enough to make most people squirm, he was no exception.

He shrank from my gaze and tried to hide behind the computer screen.

'We are not partners.' I emphasised every word separately. 'You are only alive because you are of some use to me. If you want to keep breathing, shut the fuck up and do what I tell you. Sticking your nose in my business will get you a long and lingering death. I don't care what the Council has tasked you with. They are far away. I am right here.' To accentuate my words, I took a step forward.

He flinched, actually shrinking down further behind the screen.

I turned without another word, left the house and slammed the door behind me. My sensitive ears picked up a satisfying little yelp. He was shitting himself.

Chapter Eight

And that is how we ended up in Waisland. Well, I did. I banished my little parasite to a farmhouse seven miles from town with strict orders not to show his face anywhere near where I was going. He spluttered. Resisted. Threw a tantrum. I stayed remarkably calm throughout his tirade. That finally registered with him, and he stopped his ranting.

'The Council has tasked me to watch you. All the time.' He tried to keep up his façade of self-confidence. The nervous jitter of his left eye showed how fragile it was.

'The Council wants results. What do you think they value most? That you keep an eye on me or that I stop this war that seems imminent?' I answered coldly.

'I...but...they told me to go with you.' The stutter returned. It always did when he was anxious. My calm demeanour was enough to make him flip.

'I don't give a fuck what they told you,' I continued with an edge in my voice. I took a few steps forward and forced him to retreat. He cringed and tried to make himself as small as possible. 'I'm telling you now that you are not going with me.' I towered over him. 'Your presence will endanger the mission.'

'I could help,' he stammered.

'You would fuck it up.' I didn't think I could make it any clearer. 'I work alone.' There was a hardly perceptible nod.

'So, you're going to stay here and carry on with your research.' I emphasised my words by poking him in the chest with my gloved hand. 'Or, even better, you can go back to the Council. Bring them up to speed on what we're doing here.' I smiled as I threatened to slap the side of his face. He winced and pulled back as if I'd punched him. I whispered my last addition; 'if I find you anywhere near Waisland, I will rip out your heart with my bare hands and stuff it down your throat, but not before I skin you alive.' He lost control and sobbed openly. The guy was terrified of me.

Good idea.

I'm extremely dangerous.

And he didn't even know the best of it.

Anyway, let's get back to the interesting part of this mission; Metisse.

Chapter Nine

News got around fast in this town.

I hadn't been at the restaurant table for more than ten minutes when Metisse walked up and blocked out the sunlight.

'Hello again.' His voice was warm and inviting. Deep and full of promise.

'Again?' I said in feigned indifference. I continued to scan the menu the Maître d had offered me.

He laughed; the deep sound carried over the whole room. Yeah, who was I kidding?

'Please,' he moved around the table till he stood next to me, softly picked up my hand and bowed in a dandy fashion. 'Allow me to introduce myself. My name is Metisse, and I am extremely happy to make your acquaintance.' The sparkle lit up his yellow-rimmed eyes as he lifted my hand to his lips and actually kissed the fingers.

There was no hiding his origin. The eyes gave it all away.

I smiled. There was nothing I could do to stop myself.

This guy had charisma in spades. He was even more attractive up close than he had been half naked and sweaty on the tennis court, and that had given me hot sleepless nights. He still held on to my hand, the grip soft yet unrelenting, as he righted his back. I just left it there. Even as he looked down on me, there was no uncomfortable feeling. He was imposing, but not overwhelming. Nice.

'And your name, my lady? The charm kept coming.

'Altermichan.' There was no use in giving a false name. Mine wouldn't mean anything to him anyway.

'Altermichan,' he repeated. 'A beautiful name for a beautiful lady.' Again, he bent forward and kissed my hand, this time lingering. His tongue slipped through his lips and lightly licked the knuckles. A deep heat started to swell between my legs. Wow, he knew all the tricks. Tingles ran up and down my spine, I could feel the blush starting to form on my face. His deepened smile confirmed it.

Get a grip Trish. You're here for a reason. Yeah, and he was standing right in front of me, licking my hand. I reluctantly pulled my hand from his, trailing my fingers across his palm as I left his touch.

'May I join you?' Metisse was the ultimate gentleman. Not that he expected a negative reply. I nodded, and he pulled the chair next to mine out from under the table and turned it slightly, so it stood at an angle to mine. He sat down and signalled the Maître d in an inconspicuous manner. The man rushed to the table.

'Monsieur?' he asked. Was the guy really French or just a good imitator? Whatever. The accent seemed to be compulsory for a place like this.

'Some wine please,' Metisse suggested. He looked at me. 'A dry white?' I nodded. He turned to the Maître d and cocked his head. He didn't need to specify which wine. It would be the best there was. At least he wasn't so cliché that he ordered champagne, even though a cooler with a bottle of the stuff stood on almost every table around us. I guess it was more or less mandatory here.

The Swan boasted two Michelin stars, quite an achievement anywhere, but a mind-blowing one in this vicinity. The fine linen and soft colours of the interior complemented the old colonial-style building. All nine tables were circular, seating no more than six at the largest. There was ample room between them to allow the staff to move easily between the tables as they brought the fantastic plates of food. The space also allowed for some privacy. Not that any of the other guests were minding their own business at the moment.

Soft murmuring was accompanied by quick glances our way. We would be the talk of the town by the end of the dinner.

'Your lady friend not along I see.' I smiled innocently.

'No,' he answered, matching my smile. 'She is, I'm afraid, out of the picture.' He feigned sadness, his hand on his heart. Yeah, right.

'So soon.'

He cocked his head. 'It happens.' I felt his hand move to mine again. 'I will not linger in sorrow.'

I laughed. 'I'll bet.' I let him softly stroke the fingers of my right hand. This was not lost on the other guests. I heard sharp intakes of breath. Metisse was milking it. Making sure that the congregation saw his ministrations. He was seriously narcissistic. But in a nice way.

The Maître d materialised next to him again, accompanied by a waiter holding a silver tray sporting a bottle of wine, a corkscrew and two beautiful crystal glasses. He held the bottle with the label visible for Metisse's approval, who barely glanced at it and continued to observe me. The Maître d uncorked the wine in a fluid movement that verified his many years of experience. A small amount of the light-yellow liquid was poured into one of the glasses and presented to Metisse. He finally acknowledged the wine and, taking his eyes from me, held the glass to his nose. He sniffed, enjoying the scent of the bouquet. Taking a sip, he let the wine circle his mouth before he finally swallowed.

The woman at the table across from us dropped her fork. Metisse had managed to turn the simple act of tasting a fantastic wine into an immensely seductive experience. I smiled internally. Man, he knew how to work a crowd.

'Yes, Pierre. This will do very nicely,' he said as the woman next to us stumbled to retrieve her utensil. She was beaten to it by one of the waiters. He placed a new fork next to her plate as she blushed intensely and tried not to look our way.

'What brings you to our little patch of the world?' Metisse asked, all his attention once again on me.

'Just passing through,' I said evasively.

'Not too quickly, I hope,' he was quick to answer.

'That depends.' I picked up the glass and brought it to my lips as I looked at him over the rim of the beautiful cut crystal. I took a small sip. It was fantastic, the scent full of floral aspects. The taste had a definite citrus element. Good choice, Pierre.

'Maybe I could persuade you to stay for a while.' Metisse nursed his own glass.

'And how would you do that?'

'By any means necessary,' he said more seriously than I'd expected.

Metisse was a fountain of information about Waisland and all the reasons why I absolutely needed to stay. He regaled me with stories about his family, their business and what he did for a living, which wasn't really all that much.

Different platters or exquisite food were brought to our table. We hadn't ordered anything, at least I hadn't. Every one of them was astounding. Small light bites of fantastic culinary masterpieces accompanied by yet another bottle of the beautiful wine.

Two hours later I pushed my chair back and stood up. 'A moment please,' I said passing behind his chair closer than necessary so that I brushed against his back as I passed. I felt the muscles stiffen as a result of my touch; goosebumps dotted his arms. I definitely had an effect on him. Good. That made it mutual.

The ladies' room was as luxurious as was to be expected in a restaurant of this stature. In contrast to the dining room, here everything was contemporary. Clean lines, bright surfaces with a soft, subdued light. The fresh flowers in the crystal vase scented the room nicely.

I looked at my reflection in the mirror. The wine had given me a slight blush, or maybe it was Metisse.

Man, he was a character. Sex appeal oozed out of his pores. The man was definitely a magnet, one that worked on me too. I felt hot. He turned me on no end. My body encouraged me to take him out of this place and jump his bones. But that would be a bit too quick for what I had in mind.

An idea slowly formed in my mind on how to fulfil this mission and satisfy my own agenda at the same time. It would not please everyone, but tough. But to achieve my objective I had to reign my strong and screaming libido in for the time being.

Sabretooth shifters were a strange bunch. There was no specific traditional order in the clans. There could be male or female leaders. Not like the Wolves; theirs was a male oriented society. Sabres were somewhat less chauvinistic. The strongest ruled. Giving in now would undermine any future position I wanted to have in that world. He had to chase me, while I showed my independence and strength of character.

The rest of the evening progressed in much the same way. He tried to get into my pants, and I resisted, much to his frustration and reluctant admiration. A peculiar combination. I could see he was really enamoured with me. No, it was more than that. His feelings ran deeper than just getting me in his bed. Not what I expected when I came to the restaurant.

Anyway, to make a long story short; we parted ways and I left him sitting in the restaurant. He offered to escort me home, but I had no inclination of letting him know where I lived.

The valet brought my open sports car out front as he watched from the window. I drove away and quickly left town out into the mountainous region where I easily lost the tail he'd put on me. Really?

Well, at least it proved he was very interested.

We'd see how things progressed.

Chapter Ten

He found my phone number. I have no idea how, but it just goes to show what his influence span was; pretty substantial. My phone number wasn't listed. I suspected it was the restaurant.

Metisse called me two days after we met in the Swan and invited me to a party on his yacht. He offered to send a car to pick me up, but I declined. I didn't even accept the invitation, though I knew that I would go. I just said maybe. He seemed satisfied with the answer and hung up with a cheerful 'see you tomorrow afternoon.' He was so sure of himself. Cocky even.

The next day, at three o'clock on a very sunny and pleasant afternoon, I steered the open-top sports car to the marina he'd mentioned. I hadn't expected it to be much as sailing opportunities were slim here and was pleasantly surprised the boats that lined the quay were sleek, white and obviously very expensive. This was the private marina of the upper class and it opened onto a magnificent lake. No one with less than eight figure fortunes would be welcome here. It was the playground of the local elite.

Bentleys, Lamborghinis, Porches and Ferraris lined the parking area. My E-type Jag was at least unique. I parked the deep-green Jaguar in an open spot near the entrance to the marina. I needed maximum exposure. My image would be everything in this gig, so I had to milk it. The deep growl of the engine had already gathered a crowd of admirers. When I opened the car door and swung my long, bare and tanned legs out, there were some gasps in the congregated group of men. Their attention moved from the car to the driver. Things were progressing just as I'd planned. Once again, I silently thanked my mother for good genes.

I stepped out of the car, locked it, grabbed my bag from the passenger seat and made my way on high heels to the boats. No, the shoes were not suitable for a boat, but that was not the point. I could almost hear the drooling sighs of the men as I passed.

Metisse's boat was at the end of the quay. It had to be. It was too big to fit in any of the slots. It was also where the music was coming from. Reggae music bellowed over the marina. I saw some unhappy faces on other boats, but I guess no one contemplated complaining. Hmm, another indication of the power of the Sabres here.

My arrival was noticed by the occupants of the massive sleek, white-and-yellow motor yacht. It must have been at least fifty metres in length, with multiple levels and sun decks. The striking yellow and black interior decoration was a beautiful contrast to the glossy white of the ship itself. Colourful flowers in vases and garlands completed a playful look, something the more traditional skippers in this marina must frown upon.

Metisse stood at the gangway that connected the quay

to the yacht. His face was one big smile. The bright white of his hair contrasted with the dark brown of his skin in a way that made the whole picture look mystical. His eyes flashed a yellow glow of recognition as his Sabre acknowledged me. From deep within this beautiful man, the beast made its claim. I felt tingles that started at the base of my spine. They ran up my back and at the same time slashed deep into my core, heating my body as I walked closer. I felt my nipples stiffen and tried in vain to stop them, but my body had a mind of its own. It affirmed the attraction I felt towards not only the man, but also the beast. This was a combination made in heaven. It had to be. No mere mortal could have conceived it.

I smiled.

His eyes lit up again. The yellow ochre flashed even more and stayed put for seconds. Was that a light coating of fur I saw on his bare arms? Or was I just imagining it? There was a haze, the contours of his muscled arms looked a bit fuzzy, then it receded and there was just the man. Well, "just"; the man was more than enough for now. If the Sabre had been more pronounced, I might have jumped him there and then, that was the extent of the attraction the cat had on me. I had to reign myself in for now and remind myself that I was on a mission here. Oh, yeah. The Council. That was enough to quench any erotic tendencies. Well... almost.

Metisse came down the walkway and took my hand. Once again, he brought it up to his lips and lightly kissed my fingers. The tip of his tongue slipped through his lips and licked the knuckles of my hand in a wicked way. The texture of his tongue was the rough cat's tongue. More sandpaper than subtle, but a complete turn-on, whatever it was. The cat was staking its claim again. It was a promise of what I could have. If I wanted. Hmm, let's not get into that.

'I'm so glad you could come,' he whispered. 'Please, after you, my dear.' He indicated the walkway. I took off my colourful Louboutin Cinestripes, very aware of the fact that high heels are a no-no on a maritime vessel. Not just because of the damage that the points could make to the deck, but also the difficulty it would give me personally to stay upright on a softly rolling ship. Besides, it turned out to be a super sexy action on my part. The bulge in his white shorts shouted the effect that my painted toenails, thin gold chain around my right ankle and bare feet had on him. Man, he's easily turned on. So glad I have more restraint. Yeah… right.

He followed me onto the yacht. The touch of his hand on the small of my back was light yet strong as he steered me up the winding staircase to the upper deck. It burned in a very welcome way, sending bolts of passion to my core. We passed the captain of the vessel as we walked to the space where the party was.

Chapter Eleven

All eyes turned to us as Metisse steered me towards the party. I could feel the soft growl of the boat's engine as it left the marina and slowly made its way out onto the lake. Looks like the party was complete now I was here.

The guest's reactions to my entrance varied. Some—most of the men and an occasional woman—tried to undress me with their eyes. Others stared over their glasses of Champagne with a mixture of curiosity and aggression. The last was particularly interesting.

The hairs on my arms reacted to the close proximity of the Sabres. There were more of the clan here. Many more. Though not all of those present were of a paranormal nature. There were also humans, mainly women, blonde and beautiful.

I smiled confidently, internally enjoying the mixed effect that my presence had on the gathering. I lived for this kind of thing. I guess I'm an exhibitionist at heart, or I just like baiting people. Or both. Probably both.

Metisse took two glasses of Dom Pérignon Champagne

from the waiter circling the party and offered me one. I accepted the beautiful cut-crystal glass and sipped the top-quality nectar. His hand returned to my back where it burned a hole in the sheer material of my colourful summer sheathe dress. The material hugged my body leaving almost no doubt of what was underneath. The low cut allowed Metisse to softly stroke the skin on my lower back with his thumb. It sent shivers up and down my body.

We joined a group of four, three of whom were clearly clan members. There were two men and two women. The men cast appreciative glances my way and congratulatory nods to Metisse. The blonde woman hanging on one of the men's arms was oblivious to my presence, her attention completely taken by her date. The other one, the brunette, shot killing looks my way. Ok, she was competition. The yellow in her eyes wasn't even clouded. She made her point immediately.

'Trish.' Metisse introduced the group. 'Allow me to introduce Kylian,' he indicated the man on the left, a tall, very dark-skinned man with an easy smile. Kylian took my hand and shook it enthusiastically. The smile on my face came easily.

'This is Adrian,' Metisse continued the introductions. Adrian was a large, heavily muscled Caucasian, the exact opposite of Kylian. Both were Sabres. Obviously, the clan made no difference between the race their human forms had. The cat side was what bonded. The blonde bimbo hung onto Adrian's arm and Metisse didn't even bother to introduce her. I doubt he even knew her name.

We turned to the last person in the group, the aggressive woman.

Metisse seemed unperturbed by her demeanour. I

followed suit. 'May I introduce Mariah.' She held back her hand, so I just nodded.

'Nice to meet you,' I said innocently, the smile wide on my face. She didn't react. Just stared at me malevolently.

I sipped the Champagne and tuned to Kylian who was much more interesting and friendly than Mariah, and a lot more fun. We chatted for a few moments, with Mariah fuming in the background, then Metisse steered me to the next group of people.

This continued for most of the following two hours. There must have been at least seventy or eighty people here. A small party, Metisse had said. Made me curious as to what he would mean with a big one.

The yacht stayed out on the open water for the afternoon and most of the evening. A beautiful tapas-style meal was served below decks in the captain's study. The tables were laden with beautiful dishes decorated with intrinsically carved fruits and vegetables. There were culinary delights for all tastes, with meat being the predominant ingredient. Not unexpected, with such a large feline presence.

I had a whale of a time that was nicely capped with fireworks as we slowly re-entered the marina and made our way back to the slip.

The captain moored the enormous yacht without even a bump and the gangplank was set out so the guests could leave. Amongst many "great day, Metisse", "do it again soon" and other remarks, the tipsy guests set foot on solid ground again and made their way to the cars and drivers who were waiting for them.

Metisse tried to keep me on the boat until everyone had left, but I kissed him on the cheek, thanked him for a great day, and made my way back to my E-type.

It had been a good day. Lots of fun, and a sound opportunity to see who's who in the clan. Kylian, with all his laid-back ways, was the enforcer. Adrian the finance guy. Mariah was the second-in-command as far as I could fathom. That would explain her aggression towards me. I wasn't just a challenger for Metisse's attention, I was a threat to her position in the clan as well. I'd have to keep an eye on her. She could mess up my plans.

Chapter Twelve

I called Metisse. It was time to ease up on the hard-to-get act. He'd treated me to a great day out, so I decided to give him a ring.

'Well, hello beautiful,' he answered in his soft and extremely seductive voice, sending chills to certain parts of my body again. The guy was hot. Even over the phone. Come on girl, get a grip.

'Hello, right back at you.' I matched the huskiness of his voice.

'I was just thinking about you.'

'Isn't that the coincidence?' I laughed.

'No, really, I was. Actually, you haven't left my thoughts since you stepped off the yacht and sped away in your little sports car.'

Little sports car? Was he kidding? The Jag might not be a Ferrari, but the price tag of this specific model was a hell of a lot higher than most of the cars that had graced the marina parking lot. Especially in the mint condition that

I've kept it in over the years. I bit back a reply. Not a good idea to be touchy now. At least, not that kind of touchy.

'Seriously,' he continued. 'You have been foremost in my mind all of last night and this morning. I have hardly looked at the work that needs to be done.'

'Oh my, not exactly a good influence then.'

'The best,' he laughed. Then became serious again. 'When can I see you again? This evening?'

'So soon?' I couldn't give in too much. Besides, I had things to do the coming days. Things he was not party to. 'No, sorry, not today. I have an appointment this evening.'

'Not a date I hope.' He said it in jest, but there was an undertone of panic.

'Not a date.' I relieved the tension. 'For business. I have to go out of town for a few days. Make up for the time I lost on your fantastic yacht.' I let that sink in for a moment. My cover was as a businesswoman in international finances. We'd spoken about my work yesterday on the open seas in a moment of calm while most of the other guests were either swimming or sleeping.

'How about Saturday? Surely you won't be working then?' That was four days away.

'Not if things go well this evening.'

'Then I will let you go this evening.' I let that one pass. He had no say over me, and he was very well aware of that. 'But Saturday you must come to a clan party as my guest. A birthday celebration for my mother.'

'How late and where?' I asked him. This would be the perfect opportunity to meet more of the clan and stake out the opportunities.

'My place. In the hills. Kennedy Avenue all the way up to the end. You can't miss it. We fire up the BBQ at four. Bring your swim wear, it's a pool party.'

Why did I expect the BBQ to be something more than the simple event he was trying to make it out to be? Nothing with Metisse was mediocre. Or even normal sized.

He didn't offer to send a car. That hadn't worked last time, and it wouldn't now. He was a quick learner. Good for you, Metisse.

'I'll be there.' My words were what he had hoped for. He let out his breath in an almost imperceptible sigh.

'I'm looking forward to seeing you again. Here at my home.' It was an open invitation to make it my home too. He was going fast, very fast. I must have made an even better impression than I thought. There was vulnerability in his voice. Need. He was hooked.

'Me too.' I gave him what he wanted.

Chapter Thirteen

The drive up into the mountain was worth it. The road wound between majestic forests on both sides, high embankments filled with ferns, trees and occasional flowers. Under the trees the air was cool and slightly humid. The deep tang of the fir trees interspersed with the earthy smell of the undergrowth. It was actually quite heady, and my enhanced senses took it all in, riding on a nature high. The road started to climb steeply as hairpin bends tested the E-type's versatility. It was made for this kind of environment and the deep rumble of the massive six-cylinder 3.8 engine filled the air as we easily climbed the mountain side.

The view as I turned the last corner was astounding in both directions. The vista over the mountain and valleys below with all the different tones of green, was offset in the other direction by the massive contemporary stark white building. It was a monstrosity of steel, plaster and glass and looked completely out of place in the midst of nature. The minimalistic garden held two containers with white flowers —the only embellishment visible. I don't know why, but I had imagined a stately home. Maybe even a luxury throw-back to a log cabin. Never such a modern building. I guess it made a statement, so I should have known. Metisse was a walking statement. He was the top cat in the area and everyone—absolutely everyone—would know that. Not that I'm knocking it. It's just not my taste. Minimalism is lost on me. It just looks empty.

I steered the Jag on the neatly raked gravel to the end of the small line of super-cars waiting to purge their passen-gers. Valets dressed in the same black, white and yellow that had dominated Metisse's yacht accepted the keys to the cars and whisked them away to some unseen parking. When it was my turn, I eased the car up to the asphalt at the bottom of the two steps leading up to the walkway to the house. The valet opened the door for me, and I passed him the keys as I stepped out of the car. The smile on his face was genuine. A real car lover, who clearly recognised the unique E-type. I smiled back.

Metisse was waiting for me at the end of the slate walk-way. Not surprising, I'd noticed the cameras hidden at inter-vals for the past mile. The road was the only way to reach the house, and it was heavily guarded in an unobtrusive way. Most people wouldn't have noticed, but hey, I'm not most people. In my line of work, you pay attention, or you die. It's that simple. I needed to know the layout in case I had to exit in a hurry. I was here on a mission, and Metisse, in all his glory, was one of the targets.

He reached out to me as I stepped up and took me in his arms. Quite a step up from the previous hand-kisses. His strong arms closed around me as he kissed me on the cheeks. Turning around, he left his left hand on the small of my back as he steered me into the house.

The loud music was in stark contrast to the subtle

sounds of nature that accompanied me on the trip up the mountain. It originated from the pool area behind the massive living room. The minimalistic style of the exterior was somewhat softened inside by earthy tones and the bright green of plants and strategically added yellow orchids carefully placed in groups for maximum effect. It was stunning. OK, the outside was not to my taste, but I could surely live inside.

We walked out of the living room onto an enormous deck. The white marble flooring was interspaced with tropical plants all sporting yellow hued flowers with strong scents.

The pool was something else. No straight lines there. The effect was one of mountain waterfalls that fed into countless pools at different levels on the mountain side. The water cumulated in a larger infinity pool that looked out over the mountain side. Sunken seating in the water allowed guests to sit at the cleverly camouflaged bars on either side of the pool.

Metisse took my hand and led me to the water's edge. 'I hope you've come prepared,' he said silkily.

'There's nothing that could have prepared me for that view,' I answered truthfully. It was astounding.

'There is swim wear inside,' he continued.

'That's ok, I'm wearing mine.' That brought a smile to his lips. There wasn't much material in the dress that I was wearing, so whatever was underneath was even smaller. He was right there. It was a very tasty but minuscule bikini that showed off my curves to the extreme, in a classy Dior kind of way. The tiny bits of material had cost me an arm and a leg. But I had to keep up appearances, didn't I? Besides, this was one of the expenses I was putting on the Council's tab.

So good to have a customer with unlimited funds, even if they were reluctant to part with them.

'Later,' Metisse said much to my surprise. I'd expected him to want to see me almost naked as quickly as possible. 'First there is someone that I want you to meet.' The softness in his voice made me smile.

Chapter Fourteen

The birthday girl wasn't what I expected. Metisse's mother was a regal and stately woman, proud and demanding of respect, despite the wheelchair she sat in. It was state-of-the-art but couldn't hide the fact she was unable to walk. This was a surprise. Sabres, like most shapeshifters, heal exceptionally well from any injuries. Even those that would be debilitating to humans would mend in time. Something else was going on here. More than an injury. Her legs were withered away and frail.

She looked me in the eye, curiosity as much at the foreground as the challenge to say something about her condition. I smiled warmly. Not bothering to hide my surprise. That would have been disrespectful.

'Mother,' Metisse addressed her. 'This is Altermichan. The woman I told you about.' To me, he said, 'this is my Mother, Charmaine.'

I held out my hand, careful not to bend patronisingly. She shook my hand with a strength that reminded me of where the real power lay here. She may have lost the function of her legs, but her strength was amazing. I gave back as good as I got, staying just shy of overwhelming her. This was her turf; I bowed to her.

A knowing smile lit up her face. 'Altermichan. Quite a mouthful. What are you called, child?'

'Trish,' I answered. 'I'm pleased to meet you. Metisse spoke of you often.'

'I'll bet he left out the part of my wasted legs,' she replied.

'He didn't mention that, no,' I answered while Metisse slowly coloured red.

'How did it happen?' I asked. It was best to get the elephant in the room out of the way. Gasps around me indicated it was not a subject easily broached.

'That, my dear, is a long story.' She smiled. 'One that I may tell you one day.'

I held out my left hand. In it was a small jeweller's box covered in yellow tulle and set off by a yellow and black orchid. 'Happy birthday.'

I presented the gift to her. She glanced at Metisse approvingly and took the box. Careful so as not to damage the flower, she untied the tulle and opened the box. In it was an intrinsically carved broach depicting a Sabretooth's head. It had been a gamble. A quite brazen one. She looked up from the gift and studied my face. I upheld my smile, not letting on to the feelings of nervousness that were raging through my body. Why was I so concerned about making a good impression on this woman? Sure, she was Metisse's mother. Probably the matriarch of the clan. But why did that matter to me?

The strength oozed out of her. She must have really been a force to be reckoned with when she had the use of her legs. Not that she was a push over now. Far from it. The way everyone referred to her, and tip-toed around the subject of her handicap, was tantamount to the respect that she still installed in the clan and that she was more than just the mother of the clan leader. It made me wonder if Metisse inherited the position from her instead of from his father.

She studied the delicate but strong broach. It was a masterpiece, made by a master goldsmith who owed me one. The debt had been paid in full with this work of art.

'It is truly beautiful.' She finally released me from my nerves. It had been a gamble. One that looked as though it had paid off. She took my hand again and squeezed it. 'This is such a very thoughtful gift. Something that must have kept you up at night.' She smiled knowingly. I'd have to watch it with her. There was no way I could pull the wool over her eyes.

Metisse beamed. I'd obviously done the right thing with my present.

There was a line forming behind us. All new guests who wanted to congratulate the birthday girl and pay their respects. She reminded me of the Godfather in the old films, but then a modern-day version. A supernatural modern-day version.

'We will talk later, my dear.' She ended our audience. 'And thank you so much for your gift, I will cherish it.' She took the broach and pinned it onto her scarf in a clear demonstration of acceptance. I felt relieved and quite proud of myself.

Metisse took my arm and led me to one of the bars where we both took a glass of Champagne. His eyes were filled with warmth and happiness. The smile on his face stretched from ear to ear. He bent over and kissed me lightly on the lips. Another first. He was so happy I started to believe that I had made a good impression on the matriarch.

'She's quite something,' I said. 'Your mother.'

'Yes, she is.' There was pride in his voice, but also sorrow. I left it at that. If he wanted to tell me more about the circumstances, he would.

Chapter Fifteen

The evening progressed very nicely. I was welcomed by most of the clan members now the matriarch obviously approved of me. The booze flowed easily, the BBQ was a barely camouflaged Michelin two-star meal, catered by the same restaurant we had been to earlier in the week. It was fantastic; mouth-watering. I genuinely enjoyed myself.

Metisse finally let me mingle alone, taking up his duties as the host of the party. In one of those rare quiet moments, I made my way to the ladies' room. It was more a suite; magnificent.

As with the rest of the house, the bathroom was modern but adorned with the clan colours and decorated with fresh flowers. There were two stalls and a beautiful white marble washbasin with a massive mirror. Soft towels lay folded into swans in a basket next to the sink. I entered one of the stalls and did my business. Returning at the washbasin I took one of the swan towels and placed it next to me, ready to use. I turned on the tap just as the door to the bathroom opened. In the mirror I saw Mariah enter the room. She glanced at the open stall doors and walked over to the basin. I continued to wash my hands, ignoring her dark looks.

'You're not welcome here, you know.' Her words were hard, cold. I chose not to react.

'He might be enamoured with you for the moment, but that will not last. You are nothing more than a plaything,' she continued. The tone of her voice and the way she hovered around me was threatening to say the least. I was acutely aware of the fact this could easily escalate into a major cat fight. Literally. I couldn't let that happen. It would be disrespectful to both Metisse and his mother. No way would I let it get that far. I did however have to stand my ground. She was baiting me, testing my strength.

'We'll see, won't we?' I answered, splashing water onto my chin and upper chest. It was warm outside, and the cool liquid was refreshing.

'He deserves a true woman, a real mate, not some alley-cat.' Now she was getting spiteful. Calm down Trish. Don't take the bait. 'You're a mongrel, not even fully Sabre. I can tell. There's no place for you here. You are way out of your pathetic league.' She laughed harshly.

Mariah reached out her righthand to pick up the swan next to me. She let out a gasp as I slammed my long and sharp claws down into the soft towel, stopping her from taking it. To shift here, even if it was just partially, would be seen as extremely bad manners. Disrespect towards the family. No one here showed their power.

I retracted the claws and picked up the towel, opened it and dried my hands. I turned towards her and looked her straight in the eye. She was still reeling from the breach of etiquette.

'How dare you?' she stammered. 'You cannot threaten me in this house.'

'No threats,' I answered. 'Just a clear message.' It was. She understood immediately and didn't like it.

'This is unacceptable.' She was getting a bit of her arrogance back. 'Wait until Metisse hears about this.'

'And then what?' My voice was soft, dangerous. 'Then you can explain how you threatened me. Belittled me. He's really going to appreciate that, isn't he? Especially on a day like this. At his mother's birthday party.' She was stuck. There was no way she could squeal on me without her own actions being scrutinised.

'Besides,' I continued as I put the used towel in the second basket. 'What did you expect from an alley-cat?' I smiled at her shock and moved past her towards the door. Every cell in my body was ready to fight, if need be, but I hoped she had enough sense not to do it here. I think I shocked her so much she couldn't move, anyway I left the bathroom without any further drama and made my way back to the party.

Metisse spotted me as I walked back into the living room. He smiled and started to come my way. Halfway there his expression became quizzical and he cocked his head as a fuming Mariah strode out of the bathroom and stormed out of the house. I answered his unspoken question with a shrug and another smile.

I'd made an enemy tonight. Actually, she had already been one, it was just out in the open now.

The rest of the evening was just fantastic. I had a whale of a time. So much that I even nearly forgot what I was here for. There was no way I could kill Metisse tonight. Not with the whole clan here. Besides, it would spoil a perfectly good evening.

I was one of the last to leave. Metisse tried to convince me to stay, but I declared it would be disrespectful towards his mother and he had to concede. It was difficult though. Not just for him. He took me to a remote part of the enormous house under the pretence of art he wanted me to see. There was art, only I didn't really get to see it. I was distracted.

Metisse pulled me close. I felt the heat in his body through the thin silk of my dress. Dressed in only a pair of Bermuda's and slippers, he pulled me up to his bare sculptured chest. I pressed my hands on his pecs, traced the sides of his muscles and was rewarded with more heat pressed up to my groin. His erection pushed against my lower stomach. I felt it throb. My legs were turning to jelly, and I felt a need that matched his.

Metisse slowly let his hand move from the side of my neck down over the clavicle to cup my breast. Hot flushes started between my legs and threatened to engulf my whole body. He pushed his hand underneath the material and lightly flicked my erect nipple. I groaned. I couldn't help myself. He kissed me softly on the lips. I pulled his head down and deepened it, pushing my tongue between his willing lips. His hand on my breast was driving me mad. When he came up for air he was smiling from ear to ear. His hips ground against me in a completely intoxicating rhythm. I wanted to jump him right there. Fuck the mission. Well, actually, fuck me. Please.

But I couldn't. He was a target, for crying out loud. Get a grip, girl! No, not on his boner. No. Don't. My hand moved between us as I grasped his erection through the material of his shorts. I squeezed and was rewarded with a grunt.

Metisse got his own back as he sucked on my bare nipple, sending shivers up and down my spine. He bit the hard nob lightly. Oh my God. I thought I would come right there and then. I took his head and brought it up to mine, kissing him deeply. Catching my breath.

'We can't,' I said. More to myself than to him. Saying it out loud might help.

'Sure we can,' he answered, the smile still blinding.

'No Metisse.' My voice was husky with the effort. 'It would be disrespectful to your mother. It's her evening.' I desperately needed to get some distance between us. The hold he was getting over me was definitely not in the plan. I needed some space to regroup my stupid emotions and get my attention back to the mission.

The smile faded into a pout. It was so funny and childish I had to laugh. He couldn't keep a straight face. Sulking didn't suit him, and it wasn't in his character.

'You're right. I hate to admit it,' he finally said, kissing me again. I nodded. 'But we do need to get some time alone, otherwise I will combust.' I laughed again and kissed him back.

'Tomorrow, why don't we go up to a cabin I have in the mountains. On the other side of the range. It's completely remote. We will be the only ones within miles. Guaranteed.'

In an attempt to convince me he lowered his head to my breast again and lightly bit the nipple, increasing the tension when he felt my involuntary response. His teeth expertly hovered on the edge of pleasure and pain. My resolve wavered again.

'OK, OK,' I managed to gasp as I pushed him away from me. My discipline was leaving me in leaps and bounds.

'Why don't you meet me here at six pm. I have a few things I need to do tomorrow first?' he suggested. 'Bring a small overnight bag.' His smile was sexy, promising.

I nodded as I pushed the strap of my dress back up onto my shoulder, re-clothing my heaving breast. 'I'll be here,' I affirmed as I walked backward to the door. He looked good enough to eat.

'You might want to stay here for a few minutes,' I said with a smirk as my hand closed on the door handle. He cocked his head in question.

I pointed to the enormous tent in his shorts. He looked down, then back to me. 'You sure you want to leave?' he tried a final time. His hand moved over his six-pack down to the waist band of his shorts. Slowly he pushed them down over his erection. It stood to attention and I swear it winked at me. His hand grabbed the shaft and moved slowly.

That was too much for me and I quickly opened the door and fled the room to his laughter. Man, I wanted to stay. To feel him deep inside me.

What the hell was wrong with me?

Chapter Sixteen

This wasn't me. I had discipline. Self-control. Now I felt like a lovesick idiot. I never let my emotions or feelings influence my actions. Not like this. I had a job to do. Metisse was one of my targets. He was a dead man. I had to kill him, him and the leader of the Werewolves. They both had to die to stop the prophesied war. When that was finally done, I could get around to my real mission, finding those responsible for my mother's death.

They were in the inner circle of the Council. That I knew. I was getting closer. With every successful mission, I grew my influence within the Council. The closer I got, the more information I amassed and the more they trusted me, except for Aquanaris of course. She felt there was something wrong. I avoided her where possible and made sure she couldn't touch me. One touch and she would know what I was. Maybe not who, but definitely what. And that would make me paranormal public enemy number one.

I felt I was close to the answer, very close. So why was I

endangering it all by becoming emotionally involved with my target?

Sure, I was horny. Hey, it had been a long time. And my libido was extensive anyway. But there was more. I wanted to fuck him, definitely. I almost physically needed to feel him inside me. But still. A good night's sex should be enough. I could get that anywhere.

But I didn't want to. I wanted him. I needed him.

My stupid libido, no, my emotions—even worse—were threatening my real mission in life.

I had to find a way out of the situation I was in.

Quickly.

Chapter Seventeen

Our ride to the other side of the mountain was a helicopter. Metisse piloted it. Why was I not surprised? Well, he did say that we would be alone.

The trip was beautiful as we flew over the forests and mountains. I suspect he took the scenic route so we could enjoy the trip to its fullest extent.

I love nature. And this was a great treat. At one point I saw deer running over a clearing, startled by the sound of the helicopter. The stag stopped and stared up at us, his challenge clear. He was a magnificent creature, tall and proud with massive antlers. His does and fawns rushed into the safety of the trees as he stared us down.

After about an hour, Metisse hovered over a small clearing next to a beautiful log cabin perched on the side of the mountain. I expected the cabin to be as ostentatious as the contemporary house he lived in, but it was much more modest and blended well into the landscape.

We landed and he cut the engines as I opened the door and stepped out onto the grass meadow. The house looked even better from here. Old fashioned, yet clearly very well maintained. Metisse joined me once he'd shut down the helicopter and took my hand.

'It's astonishing,' I said in awe. This was much more my thing. 'Fantastic view.'

'Yes, it is.'

We stood there for a few more minutes as I took in all there was to see. The tall fir trees, the shrubs with their red berries. The sounds of birds and small animals that carried for miles over the scenery. The owl in the tree. My sensitive ears picked up all kinds of creatures, but most of all the sound of Metisse's heart.

He softly encouraged me to leave the heavenly spot and we made our way to the cabin. Metisse picked up my minuscule overnight bag. There wasn't much use in bringing lots of clothes here. Despite my best intentions, I knew what was going to happen, and we didn't need clothes for that.

The soft twilight enhanced the feeling of belonging. Night came quickly here in the mountains, releasing the fireflies and other nocturnal creatures.

Metisse opened the door to the cabin and I saw that my initial thoughts of a small dwelling were wrong. Though cosy, the cabin was large on the inside. It was tastefully decorated with mostly Native American art and natural artefacts. Navaho blankets, sheep- and deerskin pelts were draped over robust but comfortable furniture. The kitchen was homely but very well equipped. Large windows brought the outside into the room, enveloping it in the soft twilight haze.

He turned on a few side lights, careful not to break the subdued atmosphere. His eyes followed me everywhere I went as I took in the beautiful surroundings. I was hypnotised by the view from the kitchen and stood with my back to the breakfast bar as he joined me in the kitchen.

'Would you like anything to drink?' he asked. 'Or eat?'

'You.' I surprised myself with my answer. It lit up his face. He took my hand and led me up the winding staircase to the bedroom.

All my good intentions dissolved. This could have been an opportunity to fulfil my mission. But that was the last thing on my mind.

Besides, I didn't know how to fly a helicopter.

Chapter Eighteen

The bedroom was everything I'd imagined. More square footage than a whole regular cabin, all in one room. Tall windows from the ceiling all the way down to the floor framed beautiful views of the mountains. The moonlight was more than enough light for me to see the details. My sensitive retinas bounced the light into almost daylight. I turned from the windows and let my gaze linger over the four-poster bed. Like the room, it was out of any normal proportions. Whole families could sleep here and still have enough room to spare. The silk covers and cushions invited me to jump on the bed. But it was what was on the other side that I wanted.

Metisse stood in the moonlight. His dark features warm and inviting as he smiled at me. He reached out his hand. There was no ignoring the lust I saw in him that mirrored my own. The heat in my body swelled to envelop every cell, every fibre of my being.

His touch sent shivers up and down my spine as I took his hands. He pulled me closer, into his embrace. One hand softly stroked my face and moved back to cup the back of my neck as his lips found mine. Tears welled behind my closed eyelids. Heat radiated from every part of my body where we touched. My heart thundered in my chest. I had never felt that way before, so intensely alive. I could hear his heart pounding in sync with mine. The kiss lasted forever, my tongue found his, deepening our union. Tingles followed his hand as it left my neck and passed down over my shoulder. The fingers travelled further down as they brushed the side of my breast, teasing me with what would come. Hot flashes shot from between my legs as I melted into his body. I pushed him backwards, turning him so that he fell back onto the bed. I stood over him, drinking in the sight of this gorgeous man who would be all mine in moments. My eyes must have been full of the lust that I felt to my core. His echoed what I felt, but on a much softer tone. I saw need in his face, primal need.

I knelt in front of him and placed my hands on the outside of his legs just above the knees. Slowly I pushed my fingers up, following the hard curve of his thigh muscles. Metisse's deep moan was music to my ears as my fingers spread and moved to the top of his legs, inching towards the hard bulge in his beautifully tailored designer trousers. The material strained to its limits as his engorged member pushed to escape the limitations. My thumbs rubbed the material over his testicles as the fingers closed around the big protrusion, eliciting another even deeper moan. Metisse lay back on the bed, his hands bunching the sheets as he attempted to control his lust.

The zipper gave easily as I pulled it down, the belt followed, and I released his manhood from his briefs. I pulled his pants and briefs down past his knees and over his shoes. My hands pressed his legs open and I moved forwards towards his core. I took his cock in my hands and softly let my tongue flick over the engorged head. Metisse groaned and writhed under my ministrations. I took him in my mouth and slowly let my lips move down the shaft, engulfing him in my warmth. His hands left the sheets, and I felt his fingers entwine in my hair.

He wouldn't be able to take too much of this, so I switched tactics. I stood up, and in one fluid movement I pulled up the skirt of my dress and took off my thong. I crawled up onto the bed and straddled his body, my wet core just inches from his throbbing member. He grabbed my hips and tried to push me down, but I resisted. This would be on my terms. Not his. My tempo was slower—excruciatingly slow.

His brow creased with the effort of holding back. I was driving him nuts. To tell you the truth, I wasn't doing much better myself, I just bluffed better.

I lowered myself onto the tip of his cock and started to rotate my hips a little, just enough to rub my wetness against the top of him. He went bananas. His hands left my hips and covered his head in his desperation. I continued two more rotations then plunged down. I gasped as his hot member filled me to the hilt. He cried out, grabbed my hips again and pushed even further into me. There was no more holding back, I moved up and down his shaft, helped by his hands as he picked up my rhythm. Stars exploded behind my closed eyes as I rode him. Our moans filled the room and reverberated inside my head.

Metisse grabbed me and flipped me over, never leaving my core. He plunged into me again and again. Our need dictating the speed and fierceness of our union. Heat radiated up from my core and enveloped every cell in my body. Waves of pleasure rode up from our union to my torso and my head. I felt all my muscles cramp up and let loose uncontrollably. Metisse's body stiffened and I felt him pulsate deep within me as he reached his climax. I rode it and let loose mine. I heard a cry of ecstasy that filled the room, faintly recognising it as my own. Metisse growled as he shot into me, again and again.

Spent, he lowered himself onto my heaving body as we both tried to catch our breath.

Man, that was intense. I was no stranger to sex, but this was something else. Something very, very deep.

Chapter Nineteen

My mind was confused as I lay in his arms that night. The sound of his heartbeat and the soft rhythmic breathing calmed me as never before. I felt secure there in this massive bed. In that idiotic grand building. In his arms.

I wanted to be there. Not just then, but again. More than once. I wanted to be exactly where I was—with him.

What the hell was all that about? My plan was to seduce him and get him away from his clan so that I could fulfil my mission. I was here to kill him—not to get emotionally involved. Love was a complication; one I could do without. It had never served me before and I could easily forsake all the commitment and stupid lovey-dovey stuff. I wasn't a romantic person. I was a killer, an assassin. Love wasn't meant for me. It didn't fit my lifestyle. It didn't fit my plans.

My plans went way further than just this mission.

This stint as an assassin for the Council was just a means to an end; the end of someone in the Council. I would exact my revenge for what he or she had done to my mother. For all the years we had to run and leave friends, homes and everything that was dear to us.

They took everything from me: my childhood, my innocence and the one person in the whole world I loved; my mother. I was so close to finding out who killed her it hurt. I felt the anger rise and the hairs begin to push through the skin on my spine. My fangs ached to break the skin of my gums and emerge. It took an enormous effort to stop the claws from growing at the end of my fingers. Only the steady heartbeat of my lover calmed me enough to take back control and calm my nerves.

My lover.

It sounded good. Too bad he was just a target. Him and the biker.

I could get used to his attention. He made me feel good. Important. Even loved. I knew he adored me. It was clear in everything he did and said, but most of all in his body language. Our shared heritage acknowledged each other. Spoke in a language that wasn't human or aloud. He had found his mate. It was an instinct he could not refuse or ignore. He wanted me close, twenty-four-seven. Forever.

Well, forever could be a lot shorter than he thought. Being only half Sabre gave me the power to refuse what he couldn't. I felt the pull, just as he did. But for me it wasn't all encompassing. I could refuse. I could live on without him. I could kill him.

Well, in theory.

Only it seemed such a shame. A waste of a perfectly good man. There was something about him that touched a nerve with me. He was a player, or had been, but that wasn't his essence. It was the boredom that all immortals go through before they find their mate. I couldn't blame him for that. I had done exactly the same. No, deep down inside I knew he was a good man. A good leader. A waste to kill.

So, what If I didn't?

Now that was a novel thought. If I just killed the Werewolf, then wouldn't that stop the war? And wasn't that what my mission was?

I snuggled up closer to Metisse. This newfound idea needed some thought. Some planning.

But not just now. Now, my fingers traced down his muscled chest to his six-pack, following the contours of the chiselled muscles further down to the curly hair that surrounded what I needed right now. His cock was awake before Metisse was. Ready to do my bidding. My hand closed around the hard shaft and I felt the light touch of Metisse's hand stroking my spine. I let the fur grow under his hands, exciting him even more.

There are more ways to make love if you are a shifter.

More forms.

More fun.

Chapter Twenty

We saw each other almost every other day after that. I was addicted to his body and his lovemaking. He was subtle, loving. Not like my previous liaisons. They were usually one-night stands, some with a lethal end for my partner. As an assassin I used all my talents to fulfil my missions. Sex was just another tool. Albeit it was one that I enjoyed most of the time. Men—and most of my targets were male—were so easily distracted by a flirt and a flash of soft skin. The blood immediately flowed from their heads down about a metre and that left them wanting in the thinking depart-ment. Men think with their dick. And believe me, that's not a good idea if you're on my kill list.

With Metisse, I started out using my female wiles to get close enough to be able to kill him. My strategy backfired. I became enamoured by my target. A big no-no in my line of work.

'You are my mate. You know it.' He stared at me intensely, willing me almost to agree with him. The yellow specs in his eyes glistened invitingly. Oh, it would be soooo easy to give in.

'I don't belong to anyone,' I replied, a hint of anger in the tone.

'No, you misunderstand, I don't want to rule you. I want you to rule alongside me. You are strong, it shines through you. I would never even contemplate eclipsing such strength. Together we will be unbeatable.' He tilted his head slightly to the right as he blinked those puppy dog eyes. Or should I say kitten eyes. He was after all, of the feline persuasion.

'Your mate? You don't strike me as a guy who wants to settle down.' I laughed.

'I never did. Not until the right person came. And here you are.'

'You're a player.'

'No, I was a player. You can make me an honest man.' Metisse took my hand in his, softly stroked my fingers. The light touch sent tingles up and down my spine, and heat radiated from between my legs.

'Yeah, right.'

'They were humans, playthings. Never serious contenders. You… You are different.'

'Playthings? Watch it Metisse. Your true nature is rearing its ugly face,' I challenged him.

The smile curled his lips even more, a hint of the long fangs slipped out from under his upper lip. 'Don't pretend to be insulted. I'm sure you have done the same. We are not of their lowly race. We are the top predators. And that is what we do. I'm a Sabre and so are you.'

'Am I?'

He changed tactics, still holding on to my hand. 'Which one of your parents was clan?' Metisse asked.

'My mother.'

He observed me for a minute, said nothing, just looked at me so intensely I thought he was literally trying to get inside my head. 'And she was high in the hierarchy?' Perceptive.

'The highest.'

'That figures. That's where your strength comes from.' Metisse leaned forward, his hand running up my arm to land softly on my cheek. 'There's a strange vibe with you. Something I can't exactly put my finger on.'

'Is that good or bad?'

'Good. Very good. It's mysterious. Exciting. I'm looking forward to investigating it more.' There's that mischievous glint in his eyes again. But there was more there. A longing. Maybe even hope.

'Be careful what you ask for. You might get more than you bargained for.'

Chapter Twenty-One

Talking about my mother brought back both good and bad memories.

On my way home from yet another hot evening with Metisse, the memories swamped me in the darkness of the lonely street. I pulled over and stopped the car. My breath came in gasps. Heat radiated from my body as though on fire. A sharp pain started at the back of my head just under where the spine meets the skull and quickly spasmed up through my brain, temporarily blinding me. I let it wash over me. There was no use trying to push the memories away anymore. Not now. They were here. There was no escape.

I closed my eyes, leaned my head back onto the headrest and let it all come over me.

Colourful pictures of my mother and me in a field full of flowers, laughing in a stream as I splashed her with the cold mountain water. Her warm embrace as she held me, her soft melodious voice as she sang me to sleep.

The edges of the pictures began to blacken and curl as

though burnt. An acrid smell assailed my nose. 'It's all a dream,' I said out loud in an attempt to calm myself. But it was more than that, and I knew it. The colours were replaced by blacks and browns, dirty surfaces wherever we walked. Dust and smoke. I felt my muscles seizing up, pain radiated over my whole body. Lightning flashes illuminated scenes of devastation. Blood, death, this too was my youth.

Sweat dampened the beautiful couture dress I wore as I sat in the car reliving scenes from my youth. It didn't matter. Nothing did. Only the memories.

We were running over rocks, through forests and fields. Always running, running.

'We cannot stay, my sweet,' she would tell me.

'Why not mama? My friends are here. I have friends. I don't want to go.'

'I know. Neither do I, but we must. Before we are found.'

It was always that; before we were found. Found by whom? That, she never told me until the end, just that we had to go if we valued our lives. So, we packed our meagre belongings and left by whichever means of transport we could find at that moment. In another town, in another state, we would start our lives again.

Until that fateful day.

'Run Trish.' Her voice wasn't much more than a whisper, but the urgency in her words spurred me onwards. My legs were aching, my breath came in heaves.

'Don't look back, love. Just run, as fast as you can.'

I did. I ran as fast as my twelve-year-old legs would carry me. Whatever it was that frightened my mother so much was after us. They had found us. How could this be? How could my strong and fearless mother be so terrified of what was behind us? The sound of something big rushing through the field after us pushed me a bit further. My energy was short lived. Cramp gripped the muscle of my right calf and caused me to stumble. Mother caught me and picked me up. She held me close to her chest as she ran onwards.

Over her shoulder I saw the tops of the maize undulate like massive waves in the sea. There was something there, and it was quickly moving towards us. It was catching us. I struggled to get out of my mother's arms. I needed to run myself. My weight was holding her up. It slowed her down. The stalks moved closer to us.

She let my feet touch the ground and supported me with the first agonising steps through the cramp. I bit my lip and pushed onwards. But I was too slow. Much too slow. A bellowing sound assailed my ears and chilled me to the bone. There were screams hidden in the noise. Screams of endless pain and suffering. It spurred me on with renewed energy. But still the monster was gaining on us.

I felt her hands leave my arm as she pushed me onwards. 'Keep running Trish. Keep going. Remember what I told you.' She pushed me forward. I could hear her behind me matching my steps. I ran and ran. Then suddenly I became aware that there was only one set of foot falls: mine. I couldn't feel her next to me, or behind me. 'Run my love,' she shouted. The sound came from far away. 'Don't look back. Keep running. I'll catch up.'

I crashed through the stalks, no longer moving in a straight line, just going. A faint tearing noise behind me signalled my mother had shifted. Her deep growl confirmed what I was too scared to contemplate. She was staying behind. Ready to confront whatever it was that hunted us. She would attack. She would win. She had to.

The stalks of maize disappeared and opened up into the

edge of the field. There was a forest up ahead to the right. I instinctively changed direction and rushed out of the open into the dark of the deep ferns and tangles. My foot caught on one of the vines littering the forest floor and I tumbled head over heels down an embankment into the dried-up riverbed. The deep ferns hid my bruised and battered body as I lay there trying to catch my breath. I couldn't run anymore. Not another step. Not even to get away from the monster.

The monster! Mother! Where was she? She would find me. She would follow my scent and find me.

My breathing slowed as I tried to listen. The wind through the fir trees drowned out any other sounds. I concentrated more. Just a sound, a growl, anything that would let me know that she was all right. That she was looking for me. But all I could hear were the sounds of the forest.

Darkness deepened the blacks in the forest. Even my sensitive eyes drew a blank as the canopy seemed to close over me. I huddled in the ferns and pulled my arms around my knees. Silent tears ran down my cheeks. Where was she? Why hadn't she found me yet?

The dark and fatigue flowed over me, and I closed my eyes. Just for a second—to concentrate. It was too much for me. My small body shut down as I slowly slipped sideways deeper into the soft ferns. I had to sleep. I had to... ...

Chapter Twenty-Two

A sharp pain on my right calf brought me awake. My own growl escaped my lips, and the small polecat sprang back in surprise. I grabbed a stick that lay next to me and threw it at the creature as it disappeared through the underbrush. A small trickle of blood dripped down the side of my calf from where the sharp teeth had penetrated the skin. I rubbed it away with my hand. It would heal quickly enough. I was immortal, rapid healing was one of the perks.

The sunlight shone through the canopy onto the dip in the forest where I landed the day before. The warm rays heated up the ferns and pushed away the morning dew.

'Mom!' It all came back to me in a rush of emotion. Tears fell from my eyes. 'Mom!' I called, oblivious to any danger my shouts might cause. I stumbled to my feet and scrambled up the small incline, mud and dried leaves coating my hands and knees. 'Mom, where are you? I'm here!' I cried.

I ran back through the dense undergrowth to the edge of the forest. The stark light of the sun hurt my eyes and I held my arm over them to stave off the brightest glow. I stopped at the edge of the forest. Not sure if I should continue.

There was no one there.

No sign of my mother or the monster that chased us. The only proof was the wreckage of the maize. Hundreds of stalks were smashed down to the ground forming the battleground. I willed my feet to move, slowly left the safety of the trees and walked over the snapped maize towards where I'd seen her last. There was nothing. I retraced more steps going deeper into the natural labyrinth. I called out softly; 'Mom, where are you?'

Tears streamed down my cheeks. There was no answer, even the birds were silent.

A scrap of dark green material stopped me in my tracks. She had been wearing a green sweater, the one with the roses on it. The one I gave her for her birthday, salvaged from a charity shop. This was where she'd changed, where she faced the monster of my nightmares. The echo of her last words "run, run" pained my ears. I abandoned her. I left her to die. I could at least have tried to help. I could shift. I had fangs and claws. But all I had done was run away.

My eyes were drawn to another piece of material a few metres further on. I bent down to pick it up and my hands felt the sticky liquid my sensitive nose had already identified. It was blood. Her blood. Lots of it.

My chest constricted with sobs that tore through my body. My mother was dead. She'd sacrificed herself for me. And what had I done? I abandoned her, left her to die.

My knees buckled and I fell to the ground, unable to stay upright. I hugged the small pieces of material; they were all I had left now. I was alone. My rock was gone. The one person who had always been there had been snatched from me by them.

Them. The Council.

My mind went back to the day before, when she had finally told me who we were always running from. Who and why?

It was all because of me. Because of what I was.

It was my fault.

'No, my love. No, never in a million years is it your fault.' She pulled me close, stroked my hair. 'It was my choice. Mine and your father's. We knew the consequences of our actions. Our love was forbidden. But still we continued. And now, because of their fear of us, they hunt us.'

In hindsight, I think she sensed their close proximity. That was why she finally told me about my heritage and what that meant. Why the Council hunted us so relentlessly. They were scared. Scared of me. How was that possible. I was just a slip of a girl. Twelve years old, what danger could I be to anyone?

The shaking stopped as I put the memories to rest. The pain was a dull throbbing at the back of my head that would remain there for a few more days. A trip down memory lane was always a nightmare for me. Always ending in the one question I would never get an answer to; could I have saved her?

And now I worked for the murderers of my only kin. In the classic words of Michael Corleone "keep your friends close and your enemies closer."

I didn't have any friends, so that left just them. They had no idea who I was. That was my secret. Aquanaris knew there was something about me, but obviously her "talents" were lacking as to explain exactly what I was.

No, they thought I was a shapeshifter, someone who

could change into whichever shape I wanted at will. That put me way above the single shifters in the hierarchy of the paranormal creatures. My status was much higher than that of my two targets. They were bound by their animal sides. Only able to shift to their one brother creature. The Wolves were at the bottom of the ladder, the Sabres slightly higher. Me, I was somewhere high up above the Vampires and almost parallel to the Mages.

There had been many narrow escapes when pressed for more information. I guess my prowess at what I did for the Council terminating unwanted paranormal and human elements, was too valuable to them to press the matter of my heritage any further.

Chapter Twenty-Three

Now I had Metisse safely under control, it was time to cast my attention to the second person in the war; Gabriel, the alpha of the Werewolf clan.

He and Metisse couldn't be more opposite. Metisse's world was jet set, business executives and old money. The good side of town. Of the world actually. Metisse was highly educated. He lived in opulence, servants at his beck and call. His clan was made up of influential men and women in important positions within the community.

Gabriel was the leader of a biker gang. His pack kept to the dark side of the city. They moved through the ghettos where there was abject poverty. Their world was a dark existence.

I felt comfortable in either world. Though that of Gabriel spoke to me more because it was honest. Backstabbing there was exactly that, you got stabbed in the back— literally. There was no political underlying reason for what they did. They were up there, in your face. No second agenda. What you saw was what you got. I appreciated the honesty, even if it was brutal.

Metisse's world looked beautiful on the outside but was just as merciless and rotten once you peeled away the outer designer skin. There, no one could be trusted. All had agendas of their own, all wanted to make the next step upwards. Usually to the detriment of whoever was there at that moment.

Maybe the differences went deeper than just the place in society where the two groups resided. Wolves were pack animals. All for one, one for all. They lived and breathed for the good of the pack. The alpha pair were the ultimate leaders, as long as they were strong enough. Felines were basically solitary, with the exception of lions. Sabres were a strange cross between solitary and group animals. Their hierarchy was a much more brittle one. As with the Wolves, it was based on power and strength, but not necessarily on the physical elements. They were much more political, clandestine, illicit.

Whatever it was, the two groups lived here in a rather fragile status-quo. Skirmishes around the territorial borders were dealt with swiftly and brutally, sometimes even by their own group members. Both leaders understood the importance of their peace treaty. It was the only thing that kept the two factions from annihilating each other, and any other being living in this part of the country.

This was Wolf territory and had been for centuries. The Sabres were the intruders. They settled here two hundred years ago. Their monumental superior numbers and strength quickly allowed them to carve out a substantial territory of their own to the detriment of the Werewolves. Metisse's mother, the leader of the Sabres, had chiselled out a set of rules and laws and delivered them to Gabriel's father with an ultimatum. Agree or die.

Faced with total extermination and now greatly decimated, the pack had no option but to agree. Peace was born. And with it the resentment that fuelled the Wolves. They had the short end of the stick and it showed in everything around them. The status quo was fragile—extremely so. I had to be careful whatever I did, didn't point to the other fraction that could spark off the war I was tasked to prevent.

So, how to kill Gabriel without the blame falling on Metisse?

Now that I had decided to let my new lover live, I had to make sure I was not the accidental catalyst for his death after all.

This would take some serious contemplation.

Chapter Twenty-Four

'Hello, my dear. How are you?' I recognised Charmaine's voice. I don't think I could have been more surprised. I'd picked up the phone, saw Metisse's number and fully expected my lover to be on the other side of the line.

'I hope you don't mind that I'm calling you?' she asked when I was slow with my reaction.

'No, of course not. Happy to hear from you.' It felt like I was stammering.

'I was wondering if you have plans for this afternoon?' she asked.

'I do now,' I answered with a laugh. 'No, really. I don't have anything that can't be moved.'

'Fantastic. How about we meet at the Country Club at two for a late lunch?' The Country Club. I hadn't been there yet. So, why not?

'That would be great. I'll make sure I'm there.' It was useless for me to offer to pick her up. My Jag wasn't suitable for a wheelchair. It would only make things awkward.

'Good. I will see you there. Just tell the Maître d that you're my guest.'

'Thanks. I will. See you at two.'

'Looking forward to talking to you a bit more.' With that she hung up.

OK, now that was an unexpected turn of events. Never in my wildest dreams did I expect her to contact me, or to invite me to a private meeting. It felt like an audience to royalty. I guess it was. As the matriarch of the Sabres, she had a status above all other females, above any of the Sabres for that matter. It didn't surprise me she had been the leader of the clan before Metisse. I would have to watch my step though. She was clever. She would see through any obvious lies. I had to get my act together for this afternoon.

Alex heard my side of the call and the curiosity was killing him. His eyes flitted from his laptop screen to me and back again. He opened his mouth a few times, then closed it again as he decided it might not be a good idea to ask questions. As usual, I ignored him. The guy was seriously getting on my nerves. His meddling would get him killed one of these days. Hopefully sooner than later.

I'd just experienced two fantastic days of peace while he was off to the Council to report our findings. The minute he stepped back in the door this morning the atmosphere in the farmhouse changed. I hadn't realised how irritated I'd become until he came back. Well, I'd just have to grin and bear it. There was no way Cantix trusted me enough to let me do this alone.

OK, I concede, Alex had been a smidgen helpful in finding out the initial information and guiding us here. Only now I didn't need him around anymore. Worse, he was a hindrance. I had no use for a spy.

Finally, he couldn't help himself. 'Who are you going to meet? And where?' he asked. I turned to look at him but refrained from answering. The look on his face was priceless. It alternated between disbelief and anger. Well, tough. I wasn't going to humour him with the information.

'The Council wants to know what you are doing and who you meet,' he stammered. Did this guy miss all the hints? I was not in the mood for his meddling.

'I am the official representative. You have to...' He clamped his mouth shut as I stood up and bridged the distance between us. My demeanour was unmistakable. The fur on my arms pushed through the skin, claws replaced my exquisitely painted nails.

He jumped up and stepped back, his hands raised in front of his chest in an attempt to ward me off. 'You can't hurt me,' he sputtered. 'I'm under the protection of the Council. I... ...'

'The Council isn't here,' I said softly. The ice in my voice registered and he shrank perceptively. Sweat formed on his brow and the tic in his face did overtime. He looked as though he was going to burst into tears.

'Stay out of my business, Alex. Otherwise, you just might have a very regrettable accident.' His eyes opened to the max. 'A very, very painful one.' I stared him down, literally. After what to him must have seemed like an eternity, I stepped back and gave him some room. He bolted for the bathroom where I heard him throwing up. He'd better have done that in the toilet. If he made a mess, he would be the one cleaning it up.

I left the living room with a major smile on my face. It wasn't nice of me. So what? The little bugger at least knew what his position was here. If he had any sense in that thick skull, he would get off my back for a while. He could of course go tattle to the Council. But that would probably be more negative than positive. Cantix did not strike me as the type who appreciated whiney minions.

Chapter Twenty-Five

The Country Club met my expectations exactly. An enormous white building in the middle of a golf course, perched proudly on a rise overlooking the more than forty hectares of beautifully tended grounds. The windows of the high-ceilinged building were full size, from the ceilings to the floor. Stately doors opened to a generous reception hall with windowed walls that allowed me to see right through into the restaurant and the greenroom at the back of the building. I was approached by a tall, slim man who must have swallowed a plank. He walked so stiffly upright it hurt just to look at him. He was impeccably dressed in a dark charcoal three-piece suit with an almost imperceptibly lighter grey stripe. His greying hair was practically the same shade as the stripe. The only coloured items in his whole ensemble were his tie and pocket square that were in a very tasteful lavender. The exact same shade as the accent colour of the country club. His smile was painted on. Professional; calculated to be inviting. His hands were folded together in front of his chest. As he approached, his smile deepened.

I was about to introduce myself when he beat me to it. 'Mademoiselle Trish.'

A real or a very good fake French accent.

'Madam Charmaine has just arrived, and I will escort you to your table.'

So, he knew me. Or he knew of me. I shouldn't be all that surprised. I was the talk of the town, the affluent side of town that is, due to my liaison with Metisse. There were no photos. I made sure of that. But my description would by now be general knowledge. And any Maître d worth his weight would make it his task to keep up with who is who. And probably who is doing whom. I guess I was interesting on both counts.

'Please, Mademoiselle,' he continued, 'follow me.'

He turned and walked into the main club room, past the seated groups of affluent Waisland inhabitants who openly gawked at me. I kept a radiant smile on my lips and my eyes on the Maître d, not acknowledging anyone. I suspect he took the long way to the garden room as we weaved in and out of the restaurant to make the best of the drama. Showing me off to the members. It was so chauvinistic and petty it was almost funny. Almost. I had to stay in character, so I just kept on smiling.

We finally entered the gigantic conservatory.

It was magnificent. Wrought iron and facetted windows opened the room up to make the best of the beautiful lake view at the back of the Country Club. I hadn't seen that detail when I drove up. The effect was sublime. Every iron strut was decorated with beautiful fresh flower arrangements in cut crystal vases that stood on one-metre-high marble columns.

The wall that linked to the stone part of the building was painted in the lavender and soft light green colours that gave the club its name: The Lavender & Lime Country Club. It was a throwback to the last century when this area had been full of deep purple lavender fields for the production of perfume.

The deep rattan chairs with the same lavender and lime shades in the thick cushions around low glass coffee tables looked extremely comfortable. A little closer to the windows the club had placed dinner tables and high-back chairs in the same design. The undercarriages of the glass tables were dark olive-green bronze sculptures of animals. What could have been cliché was extremely chic. The balance perfect.

Charmaine sat at the best table in the house.

Situated near the window it boasted an unobstructed view of the grounds. There was one additional chair, for me. It was placed at an angle to Charmaine so we weren't completely opposite each other and could both enjoy the view.

The Maître d singled to a waiter who rushed over to take my light summer coat. Another man materialised and pulled my chair back ready for me to sit down. First, I wanted to greet Charmaine.

'Hello Charmaine.' I walked over to her and offered my hand. She amazed me once again by moving the chair out and up so that she could kiss me on the cheeks without me bending down. Face was everything here. There was no way she was going to have anyone tower over her. It was all in the details.

'My dear,' she acknowledged me for all the prying eyes to see. 'I'm so glad you could come. As always it is good to see you.' You could have heard a pin drop. All eyes were on us. People here sure were nosey.

I moved back to my chair and sat down as the waiter

pushed it forward for me. Charmaine returned the chair to its normal seating height with a soft whirr and moved her legs under the table.

The Maître d took the bottle of white wine out of the cooler, dried the bottom with a white brocade cloth and presented it to me. It was a beautiful New Zealand Sauvignon Blanc. I nodded, and he poured a small amount of the pale yellow-white liquid into the crystal glass. I took a sip, not bothering with all the pooh-ha of smelling and swigging the wine. I liked it or I didn't. I wouldn't pretend to be a connoisseur; I'd never be able to pull it off. The wine was sublime. A beautiful citrus taste that was refreshing. I nodded my appreciation and put the glass down. He poured again and placed the bottle back in the cooler.

'Thank you for making my son so happy.' Charmaine was definitely to the point. I think I blushed because she laughed.

'He makes it so easy,' I replied.

'He is very enamoured with you. I don't think I have ever seen him so much in love.'

I had no answer to that. Mostly because of the nagging feeling that I was a fraud. I started to feel uncomfortable. I didn't want to deceive either Charmaine or Metisse, but I wasn't who they thought I was. True, I had feelings for him. Deep ones. Enough to make me change my mind on killing him. Still, I knew his commitment was much deeper than mine.

'I don't want to make you uncomfortable, my dear.' Charmaine covered my hand with hers, squeezing slightly to emphasise her words. She leaned back in her chair. 'I hope you will be around for a long time.' It wasn't posed as the question it was.

'I don't have any plans to leave in the near future,' I

answered with a smile. 'Though I may need to take short business trips every now and then.'

She nodded her assent.

The Maître d hovered to the right of the table. Charmaine smiled her acknowledgement.

'My lady, shall I have the lunch brought out?' he asked in a subdued voice.

'Yes please, Jean.' The lunch? So, it had already been decided what we would eat. No secret where the power lay here.

He signalled to someone behind me and no more than thirty seconds later, a platter of exotic salads and fruits was placed on the table along with delicate finger sandwiches. Cold fish and meats rounded up what I thought was a fantastic spread. The smell of the fresh ingredients was amazing. Nothing was overwhelming, all the scents stood out individually. The platter was decorated with edible flowers and carved fruits. It was truly glorious.

The waiter stayed at the table, unsure whether he should serve us or not. Charmaine waved him away in a friendly manner. We would help ourselves.

'Please,' she indicated the food. 'Enjoy.'

'That I will,' I answered honestly.

It tasted as good as it looked. Fresh flavours, delicate spices, home-baked bread. All to Michelin standards. I ate much more than I had planned. I couldn't help myself.

We chatted between bites. Mostly about me and what I did for a living. I spun the carefully constructed story. It would all be backed up on internet, thanks to Alex.

Charmaine told me more about Metisse, his childhood, education and his responsibilities in the family businesses. It was very interesting. Many of the blanks Alex and I ran into while researching were filled in. Not that I was planning on telling Alex. I kept him in the dark as much as possible.

My doubts about the mission grew every day I was in Waisland and amongst the Sabres. The information Cantix and Aquanaris gave me had more holes in it than Swiss cheese. Alex tried to strengthen the lies, but he was so obvious it was pathetic. He was a bad liar. A bad almost everything, to be honest.

We finished lunch with coffee and homemade praline chocolates.

Charmaine folded her napkin and manoeuvred the electric chair out from under the table. 'Walk with me,' she requested as she moved towards the door connecting to the grounds. A woman and a man who had quietly been sipping coffee at the table next to us during our lunch, stood up and followed us at a discreet distance as we made our way out of the conservatory onto the Country Club gardens.

Someone as important as Charmaine never travelled anywhere without security.

Chapter Twenty-Six

Once we were out of the busy club's earshot, Charmaine raised the seat of the chair so her head and mine were at the same level as we moved over the winding path.

'Thank you for that,' she said. I looked at her to gauge what she meant. My quizzical features caused her to smile.

'The whole show for the club's members,' she explained.

I smiled myself. Yes, that was what it had been about. A show. One to let everyone know she acknowledged me as her son's girlfriend and an official member of the family.

'Thank you,' I answered. 'For welcoming me that way.'

'I meant what I said,' she continued. 'You make my son very happy. He has searched for his soul mate for a long time. I think he had essentially given up before he met you. He deserves to be happy.'

I refrained from an answer. None was required.

'I sense there is more to you than meets the eye.'

Oh shit, this was where it would start to get hairy.

'You have depths that my son does not see. There is a single-mindedness and focus about you. I believe you have a goal, and I would like to know if Metisse is part of that.'

She was to the point.

'He is,' I answered truthfully, though not expanding more than that. She didn't push, just let the silence do its work. I, however, am just as proficient in the use of silence and so not easily intimidated. I left it at that.

She looked at me and smiled. 'I trust you Altermichan.'

Why my whole name? Was it to make a point? How much more did she know about me? The tingles running up and down my back made me feel it was more than I wanted. There was no real obvious reason why she should trust me. She hardly knew me. She didn't strike me as the kind of person to rely on her intuition alone.

'You will do what is right.'

What the hell did that mean? This meeting was becoming more complicated and frustrating with every step I took. I decided silence would probably be my best option for now.

'Do you remember when we first met?' she broke the silence. 'At my birthday party?' I nodded. 'I was very impressed you didn't try to hide your surprise at my physical handicap. Most people pretend there is nothing out of the ordinary. They avoid looking at me or my legs. I find that extremely irritating. You were a breath of fresh air. I like your directness.'

We walked on past the pond and the beautifully tended water plants. Colourful ducks swam on the crystal-clear water and herons fished between the water lilies.

'The clan was pushed out of Canada by the Council,' Charmaine continued.

The Council again. We seemed to have more in common than I thought.

'We were too powerful for them and their solution to such problems is to decimate the threat. Many of my people were killed in the fights that ensued when they attacked us. We were a peaceful community, and our defences were minimal. I blame myself for that. We were complacent.' There was anger in her voice.

'The only option left was to flee. The clan crossed the border, and we came here, hoping to distance ourselves from the long reach of our enemies. The reprieve was short-lived. They found us within a year and attacked again.'

The story was taxing her. I felt the tension in the air between us. She was angry and her aura let off sparks.

'There was a young wizard,' she continued. 'He was exceptionally powerful. He managed to bring a small party of assassins and wizards into our new territory and threatened to kill our young. There was no depth they would not sink to in order to bring us back into their fold. My family and I were all that stood between the wizard and our cubs.'

She stopped the chair and turned to face me. Her eyes blazed with the anger I could physically feel. 'The fight was terrible, bloody. There were casualties on both sides, mostly on theirs. We had the upper hand because of the terrain. Sabres are ambush hunters, and we were in between the trees in the dark. There was little moonlight and the lamps they brought didn't pierce the darkness. We almost triumphed. Only the young wizard and two assassins were left in a small clearing. We surrounded them and moved in for the kill. The wizard identified me as the leader and cast a terrible spell. I went down, my body convulsing in the curse that ate away at me. The pain was more than I could take.'

The story visibly taxed her. 'The clan faltered. I was writhing on the ground. More of my body shut down with every wheezing breath I took. I should have died. I nearly did.'

'How did you survive?' I asked.

'There was someone else there. An age-old power. He intervened. The wizard and one of the assassins escaped in a cloud of smoke as soon as they saw him, the last one wasn't so lucky and died at his hands. Then he transferred his attention to me. He managed to keep me alive and to stop the ravage the spell wreaked on my body. My legs he couldn't save. That was the price I paid that day. I did so willingly.'

'Who was he?' I inquired. Something inside of me tried to remember something. It eluded me. I had no idea what I was looking for in my memories. I hadn't encountered anything like this before, so how would I know to remember?

She didn't answer. Just stared at me with those blazing eyes. It unsettled me even more. I sensed she wouldn't tell me whatever I did. Not now. Maybe later.

I tried a different question. 'Have they been back? The Council?'

'No, they haven't.' She said it slowly. Letting every word land. Did she know about my mission? I became more and more convinced she knew or at least suspected something. That just complicated this job a thousand-fold.

Shit.

What the fuck was I going to do?

Carry on with what you're doing now. The voice inside me urged. I was in this too deep now to just stop. Besides, I wasn't actually doing what the Council asked me to do. There were too many doubts. And they had just been boosted.

'They will come back for another try, and then we will be ready,' Charmaine added.

Chills went up my spine. I had to stop myself from shuddering. We looked at each other for what seemed like a long time. It was probably no more than a few seconds, but the intensity made it seem like eternity.

Then she smiled. 'But enough of that,' she said as she took my hand. 'I trust you will do the right thing, my dear. And that ours will be a long-lasting friendship.'

If that was supposed to make me feel better, it wasn't working. It actually scared the shit out of me. No pressure, right. Only I had no idea what I was supposed to do, what was expected of me.

'Now,' she said as she turned the chair around and started back up the path to the Country Club. 'I have taken up enough of your time. You have better things to do than listen to the ramblings of an old woman.'

'There is nowhere I would prefer to be than right here, right now,' I answered.

Her laugh was warm and full which complicated things even more.

I was lost. I had no idea how to process what had just happened.

I needed some time to figure it out.

We circumvented the busy building and went straight to the parking area. A big black van was already parked there with its rear doors open and a ramp ready and waiting for Charmaine. The vehicle was sleek in a menacing way. The interior was customised to the fullest with the upholstery in the clan colours. The driver, another Sabre, stood to the side of the ramp, ready to help in case he was needed.

'Thank you for our little talk.' Charmaine took my hand again.

'Thank you,' I answered. 'For the wonderful lunch and your openness.'

'You are very welcome.' I knew she meant it. 'And always will be.'

With that she drove the chair up the ramp and was swallowed into the vast cavern of the vehicle. The driver pressed a button somewhere and the ramp disappeared into the van as the doors closed.

I turned, retrieved my summer coat from the busboy who stood waiting and made my way towards my Jag.

My mind raced at a thousand miles an hour.

Chapter Twenty-Seven

I didn't get it.

It was so confusing.

I was sure she knew a lot more about me, and why I was here, than she should. And still she trusted me.

Or was it all just bullshit? And if so, what kind of game was she playing? The really ridiculous thing about all this was that I actually believed she was sincere. How's that for a conundrum.

Let's just assume she's genuine. Then what could she know about me? She could have spoken about me with Metisse. Or maybe had someone do a search on the net. That avenue wouldn't have landed her any more information than the smoke screen Alex had put up.

It was bullet proof. He spent most of his day perfecting my image of a jet set businesswoman. He sent and answered mails. Booked trips I would never go on. Rented villas in exotic places under my name. All in case someone started researching me as meticulously as we researched Waisland.

I had no idea how to continue with Charmaine. Not a clue. I could hardly ask Alex for advice. He would go and pass it on to the Council immediately. I don't think they were actively looking for Charmaine anymore, not after they'd wounded her and she'd mentioned they presumed her dead, but I couldn't take the chance.

Something kept nagging at the back of my mind. I couldn't get a grip on it. Not in the drive to the farmhouse, and not during my run through the fields and meadows that afternoon.

I stood under the hot shower and enjoyed the searing hot drops of water as they cascaded over my skin. Then I turned it to ice cold. Shivers ran up and down my back. The cold felt like sharp shards of glass until I got used to them. That was my cue to turn on the heat again. I loved it. It invigorated me. After a ten-mile run, this was the ideal way to recuperate.

I finally stepped out from under the shower onto the plush bathmat. I grabbed my king-sized towel and started to dry myself off when it suddenly hit me what had been bothering me all this time.

I dressed and went into the living room where Alex was glued to his laptop again. The guy never left it. He was a wizard geek. The first one I'd ever encountered.

He looked up, startled. He always felt my eyes on him and that made him very nervous.

I sat down in the chair opposite him. His tic started again. This gig must be hell for the little guy. I was almost sorry for him. Almost.

'Alex.' He jumped visibly

'I have a few questions for you,' I continued. He nodded quickly, the tic in his eye still going strong. 'Aquanaris is the Oracle, right?'

'Yes,' he answered warily, not sure where this was going. 'What kind of things can she see?'

The surprise temporarily stopped his tic. I think he was about to ask me why I wanted to know but decided against it at the last moment. Smart move, I wasn't in the mood to discuss my reasons with him.

'She sees the future,' he started. 'And she keeps track of all paranormal creatures.'

'All of them?' What, like some kind of Cerebro from the X-men? Now that would be frightening in the hands of the Council.

'Not individually,' he explained. 'But she does see groups and can say what they plan to do now and in the future. That is why we are sent to stop rebellions before they start.'

Hmm, that word "rebellion" again. It was a slip of the tongue and Alex coloured bright red when he realised what he'd said. I chose to ignore it, as if I hadn't heard. Relief flooded his face. The man was really naive. It would get him killed one of these days.

'So, she can see communities of paranormals and pinpoint any trouble that may be brewing there?'

'Yes, like she did with your mission.'

'Ah, yes. And that brings me to my question.' He was all ears. 'If she can see groups, how come we had to do the research? Wouldn't she have seen that we had to go to Waisland? That the clan and the pack here were the ones we were looking for?'

He looked genuinely surprised. The cogs in his mind creaked as he processed what I just said.

'You'd think. Wouldn't you?' I said in a completely unthreatening manner. I didn't want him to get his antenna up. If he knew what I wanted to know, badgering him wouldn't help. 'I mean, it took you a long time to find this place. Even you.' I piled on the compliments. 'It was hours and hours of dedicated research. You nailed it. Of course, you did. But how come you knew, and she didn't?' This was bordering on sickening, the way I was sucking up to him.

'Yeah,' he finally answered. Just in time, before I lost my cool and decided to try and beat it out of him after all. 'You would, wouldn't you?'

I let him talk.

'It took a lot of work. Lots of deduction on my part.' He conveniently forgot it was me who chose Waisland in the end, despite his protests. I just nodded and smiled slightly. 'Aquanaris can see almost all of groups or locations. But some are hazy. Like they're in a cloud. She can't focus on them and see what they're up to. I tried all the regular groups first, then went to the list of hazy areas. That's when I came up with Waisland.'

'And Waisland is in one of those clouds?'

'Yes. It is.'

'Where do the clouds come from? Why the haze? I thought she was all-seeing.'

'We don't know. Maybe some remnant of an old magical settlement. Atmospheric turbulence. Could be anything.'

Yeah, I thought. Maybe even someone who is adept at pulling the wool over the Council's eyes.

'Why?' he suddenly asked.

'No reason. I was just wondering.' I shrugged my shoulders, stood up and went to the couch where I took the remote and started zapping through the channels.

Chapter Twenty-Eight

How to get to know the other target? The Werewolf. The one who would have to die now that I'd decided to pass on killing Metisse.

Gabriel was the alpha of the Werewolves in Waisland. They were a large pack, bigger than most.

Generally, a pack consisted of between six to ten Wolves. Some were larger with twenty to thirty. The Waisland pack had closer to forty members. Their territory to the south and east of Waisland was a lot more extensive than other pack's. It had to be, to be able to sustain such large numbers and still keep the secrecy that was paramount to life itself. The abundance of prey in the forests around Waisland contributed to the growth in a major way. Werewolves in rural areas had a harder time hunting undetected by humans.

The only other large predators in the region here were the Sabres. Their presence frightened away any other kind of feline from their territory north of Waisland.

Both super-naturals were the apex predator in their

area. The Wolves and the Sabres lived in a fragile coexistence. Traditionally they were enemies, competitors for the same territory and food, but they usually steered clear of each other.

The Sabres came from Canada. That much I'd heard from Metisse and Charmaine. They were the invaders, maybe that was the cause. But if it was the Wolves' territory, why the status-quo?

The Sabres lived in the good side of town. The Wolves didn't.

There were more differences than just their origins.

As I was about to find out.

Chapter Twenty-Nine

My arrival in what was generally called the bad side of town caused quite a stir.

The deep thump of the big two cylinders attracted a lot of attention as I slowly let the bike rumble down South Main Street on a radiant Sunday morning, just as the good people of Waisland emerged from the stark white chapel at the end of the long straight road.

Maximum effect. Exactly what I wanted.

The collective congregation stopped their conversations and simultaneously dropped their bottom lip to stand and gawk at what just entered their God-fearing town.

The supple leather that hugged my legs and hips was in stark contrast to the homely and prudish long skirts and high-necked blouses of the female church goers. The tank top shirt and short leather jacket finished my look.

Even the old priest, who must have seen it all before, was dumbstruck. He clutched the bible closer to his purple and gold vestment and mumbled some prayer or incantation.

his groin. The sound of the thud rang loud in the unified silence that followed my invasive move.

My would-be assailant's breath whooshed out of his mouth as a silent scream began to form. It never left his lips. I kicked him in the jaw as he doubled over, his hands grabbing at his wounded groin. He went out for the count.

The room was silent. You could have heard a pin drop. No one even breathed. The bikers looked at each other, unsure how to proceed. I waited patiently. I stood my ground and looked them in the eye. There were more red-laced eyes now, more fur pushing through. Lust had quickly turned to anger. They finally made up their collective mind and one by one they stood up from their chairs and started to advance towards me. All except one.

'No,' he said without raising his voice. As one they stopped their advance.

OK. This was the guy I had been looking for. The one my small demonstration had singled out. The pack alpha. I smiled again.

One of the guys was reluctant to stand down. I felt the tension. Felt and read the body language. Would he defy his alpha? Now that would be interesting.

The alpha stood up and casually left the dark corner where he had been sitting to walk over towards me. He was all I expected, more than I hoped.

Now it was my turn to be impressed.

He was almost as tall as the guy I knocked to the ground. His wide shoulders held a mass of muscle that flowed easily into the large biceps of his arms. A broad chest strained at the black T-shirt stretched to almost breaking point. His waist was tapered. His jeans covered well-muscled thighs that pulled the material when he stepped forward. Tough leather boots finished the picture.

Not that my eyes went anywhere that low. I got side-tracked by all the muscle between the neck and the knees. I do love a well-muscled man.

He stopped about a metre in front of me. Clever. Out of reach of my knees. I smiled, more at the impression I had made than towards him. He smiled back, kind of. His lips stayed closed, just the edges curved up slightly. Most of all, his eyes shone.

Chapter Thirty

The guy was handsome. Even more so up close. His dark features, long black hair and sparkling eyes struck a chord with me. Not so much my heart—I'm not like that—but any other emotion just skyrocketed. Especially the hot ones. This guy pushed my buttons, and he hadn't even spoken to me yet.

'So, what are you doing here?' His voice was deep, warm, with an edge. 'If you're not here for a lay, what then?'

'Never said I wasn't.' Maybe not the best reaction, but what the hell. The attraction was clear and present in the electricity that filled the air between us.

The smile widened and his stark white teeth showed. Even, solid choppers; the incisors slightly longer than a normal mortal's. But then. This was no mortal. This was the alpha of the Waisland Werewolf pack. His pack was legendary. They were strong, held their massive territory against rival packs and ruled the woods. Well, most of the woods. The rest and the mountains belonged to the Sabres. Metisse's clan.

There was an uneasy truce between the two and I was about to test it to its limits.

'It's hot out.' I thought I'd change the subject before I jumped his bones right there and then. 'The sign said beer and the bikes out front indicated it was my kind of dump.' I shrugged my shoulders in what I hoped was complete nonchalance. His deepened smile belied that. Well, it was worth a try.

'That it is,' he answered. 'Hot in here too.' His gaze travelled down from my face over my breasts, down past my naked bellybutton with the shiny piercing and on to the leather pants. The temperature inside just shot up by more than ten degrees. Thank God I was wearing my leathers. Any jeans would have advertised the arousal I was feeling right now. And this lot had sensitive noses. As his eyes roamed back up, they lingered on the hard nipples that poked through my shirt. Shit. There was no hiding those.

'Get the lady a drink,' he called out. 'Come sit with me.' He turned and went back to the corner where he sat when I came in. It was darker there, cooler, not that I noticed. His left hand pulled a chair out from under the round wooden table. For me, I guess. Being the good girl I am, I took the seat.

The bottle of beer that materialised in front of me was frosted, beads of water painted a trail as they slowly moved down the glass to pool on the table surface. It looked so inviting. I slowly picked it up, unscrewed the cap and put the lip to my mouth. I tilted the neck a little and let the cold liquid slowly flow down my throat. Man, that was good.

I heard a chuckle to my left and turned my head slightly

to observe the alpha. 'I needed that,' I said very redundantly.

'Yeah,' he answered amused. 'Cause it's hot outside.'

We sat in silence for a few minutes. I was thankful for the short reprieve and attempted to get myself back under control.

'When did you arrive in town?' he finally broke the silence. I turned my head towards him and placed the almost empty bottle back on the table.

'Today.' Small white lie. But hey, I didn't see him getting to the "good" side of town any time soon. I guessed I could get away with being less than honest. Besides, the person I was now, had just arrived. The one Metisse knew was a totally different me.

Every now and then his lips twitched ever so slightly as he drew in a deep breath. Still trying to get my pheromones, huh? Well, good luck with that.

'Just passing through?'

'That depends on what I find here.' I picked up the bottle again and drowned the last of the liquid.

He lifted his right hand for a moment and then placed it back on the table. New bottles of beer appeared on the table and he pushed one my way.

'Maybe I can give you a reason to stay,' he joked.

'And what would that be?'

'You're looking for your mate.' He was direct. No beating about the bush here.

'Maybe.' I drank again, to let it sink in. 'And what makes you think I'll find him here?'

'You already have.'

That had to be the shortest courtship ever. Bit too quick for my liking. OK, my body was screaming at me that I could at least try him out and see, but I'd just have to ignore that.

Giving in so easily would endanger my plans. It would solidify his position as the alpha, as my pack leader and me as the submissive pack member.

Nope. Not going to happen. Didn't fit in the image I had of the future. I just smiled sweetly.

'Yeah, well then, I'd know, wouldn't I?' I alluded to the imprinting that was the bane of the werewolf. A mind-blowing attraction between a male and female wolf that pulled them together from the first moment they met. There was no denying the imprint. To try and ignore the attraction would make them physically ill.

'You do.' He was so sure of himself.

'We'll see,' I said as I drowned the last drop of beer from the bottle and stood up to leave.

His hand felt hot when he took my arm. I felt tingles up and down my body, mainly down. 'You can't fight it,' he emphasised.

I just smiled my answer. I reluctantly disentangled my arm from his heated grip, nodded to him and made my way back out of the small building to my bike.

The bright sun and the heat hit me like a two-by-four. I hadn't realised how cool it was in the bar, nor how dark. My eyes had adapted to the lack of light, another plus for my heritage.

I blinked and pushed my sunglasses back down over my eyes from the perch they had on top of my head.

My gloves were still on the bike's seat where I left them. That's a fickle thing I have. I always wear gloves when I ride the bike. Whatever the temperature. It has to do with road rash. Sure, I heal a lot quicker than humans, but it's still painful and highly unpleasant, so why run the risk. Helmets

I discard. Too stuffy. And not good for the image. There's something about long red tresses riding the wind that attracts men. These kind of men. I put it down to a necessary risk.

The bike started with a deep rumble. The sound comforted me. Like a massive beast's heartbeat. I love the power it lets me feel. The strength. It's a close second to the way I feel after the change. Only more acceptable in the human world.

I pulled the bike upright, folded the kickstand in with my foot, kicked the bike into first gear and rode off. There was no need to show off any more than I'd already done.

I'd achieved my goal. I stirred feelings in the alpha of the pack. Feelings he would not be able to ignore. I knew it would be him. Who I was, dictated only the best would be good enough, and he was it. Images of future encounters started to fill my head. I have a lively fantasy and this hunk of a man had truly inspired me.

He would be feeling a lot more than attraction. Imprinting was a miracle and a curse to the lupine kind. They risked certain death by ignoring the call. So handy that I wasn't susceptible to that side of the coin.

Only he didn't know that death was the outcome, whatever he decided.

Now all I had to do was wait for a few days, until the need within Gabriel reached unmanageable heights. Then I would show my face, and body, again.

Chapter Thirty-One

I watched from a distance. The parking lot at the bar was full of bikes. Many of the riders lined up outside the doors, milling around. Nervous looks were exchanged. Every now and then I heard a loud crash from inside the bar, just before another unlucky pack member tumbled out of the doorway. Finally, Gabriel stood in the opening. His dark features were haggard. Deep bags under his eyes testified to the lack of sleep. The bright red of his pupils was a dead giveaway he was fully into the imprint misery.

It had been three days since my memorable first and only visit to the pack. And man, had I turned this lot on their heads. It was all progressing exactly as I planned. It was time to make contact again. I needed him to be desperate, but not in a way that he would do anything really stupid.

I had to be careful. Gabriel was extremely volatile now he was battling the imprint.

He had remained quiet for the first day. The pull was

there, but it was manageable. Then the full moon threw all his resolve and restraint out the door.

I'd timed my arrival well. The lunar cycle enhanced the imprint's effect. It was full moon now and would be for another night.

He was rapidly losing the fight.

Gabriel sent his acolytes out to find me. They roamed the south side of town, one even dared to move over the boundary in the deep of the night, but only just. A few blocks, no more. That was Metisse's territory. The pack was not welcome there. Trespassing would be punished with at least a massive beating. Any intrusion into the other's patch might spark off an unprecedented violent reaction. One that would bring the whole town down with it. Humans and all. That was not in the plans.

I had to diffuse the situation before it got out of hand.

I retraced my steps through the forest from where I had observed the bar, got into the car and made my way out of the woods. Once at my safe house I changed clothes, started the bike and drove off in the opposite direction to Waisland. I wasn't ready yet to let anyone know where to find me. A diversion was in order.

Two hours later the deep rumbling of the bike broke the tranquillity of the church grounds on the south side of the small town.

I parked the bike outside the church, sat down on a bench and waited for what would happen. The distinct sound of the big twin had been heard down the road at the pack's HQ and it was just a question of time before they came to investigate.

Sure enough, a chopper appeared at the end of the street, the rider stared in my direction. He took out a mobile and held it to his ear. I couldn't hear what he said. He replaced the mobile back in his jeans and waited, the bike still idling, probably in case I decided to skedaddle again. Now that would be fun. A high-speed chase. But no, not now. Things were too volatile for fun and games.

Another bike thundered up to the sentinel. Gabriel.

My legs momentarily turned to jelly, just as well I was seated. I can fight imprinting, no problem. But that didn't mean I wasn't susceptible to the charms this guy has.

The heat spread from between my legs up through my body to stiffen my nipples. I tried in vain to control my body and stop the pheromones from broadcasting what I was feeling. A bit was okay, but not too much. I had to stay in control. Every metre he came closer made it more difficult. I closed my eyes and let my head rest on the back of the ornate carved bench. The sun beat down on me and helped me order my emotions. I was here for a reason, remember.

The bike pulled up in front of me.

The resonance of the big engine travelled up from the street through my legs to my overheated groin. I heard the kick stand being extended and the bike shut off as Gabriel let it slant to park.

The sound of his boots on the gravel, and then on the grass filled my ears.

His scent attacked my nostrils; heavy musk came off his tormented body.

I finally opened my eyes and let them travel up the beautiful macho man in front of me. From the tight jeans, over the bulge at the fly, past the six-pack and the massive pecs to his dark burning red eyes. The heat in my core almost pushed me over the edge. He had a hell of an effect on me. Lust, pure lust. I wanted to jump his bones, rip his leather jacket, open his jeans to free the erection that was pushing at the zipper and feel him in me.

But that would have ruined the moment.

So, I just sat there and waited for him to make the next move.

Chapter Thirty-Two

We left the church grounds on the bikes. I followed him without a word. Let him lead me to where we would be alone. His need had to be met. Now, before it engulfed him even more—to breaking point.

We stopped at a house. I didn't notice anything more than the door that led us inside. I was completely absorbed with Gabriel.

What the fuck was happening? First Metisse, now Gabriel. My libido was doing overtime. It ruled me, my thoughts, my actions.

This was not me. Yet it was, in some perverted way. This was exactly where I knew I should be at this time.

There was no need to wait anymore. I had him exactly where I wanted him. He was mine. There was no way he could deny the attraction and live. He acknowledged as much by bringing me here. This was on my terms.

I pulled him towards me. My hands moving over his pecs, down to the six-pack. Then further. To the turquoise and silver buckle on his belt. I pulled it loose, zipped the fly down and stuffed my right hand down his jeans, my fingers closing over his hard member. His hands grabbed at my tank top, ripped the material and he cupped my breast in his rough calloused left hand. The other one held my face as he kissed me hotly.

His jeans dropped to the ground. He stepped out of them and picked me up. I wrapped my legs around his waist, his throbbing cock pushing at the supple leather of my pants, the only thing that held him from what he so desperately needed.

Gabriel swiped the kitchen table clean with one arm and laid me down on the cool white surface. I reluctantly relaxed my legs and let him step back slightly. His hands unzipped my pants and pushed them down my hips as I arched my buttocks off the table.

In one fluid motion he yanked them down my legs and over my boots. I was naked underneath the leather.

Both of us went commando. Who knew?

Well, it was handy now. He spread my legs, his hands stroked the tender inside of my thighs and sent tingles up my spine.

Slowly, ever so slowly, he moved up my inner thighs towards the hot core between my legs. The light fluttering touch of his fingers belied the urgency of his need. He had more restraint than I'd ever imagined. I was now the one at risk of losing any last discipline I thought I had. His fingers finally found the wet nucleus of his dreams. He pushed his finger into me as I cried out in utter pleasure.

That, and my scent, pushed him over the edge and he grabbed my hips, plunging his throbbing member deep into me.

I screamed now in earnest as he lunged deep into me

again and again. No restraint, no holding back. Plain and pure need on his side and lust on mine.

I felt the heat swell from my core out to my nipples, up further to my neck and face. It engulfed me as I rode the orgasm to the fullest. Again, and again, the waves rolled over me as he continued to ravish my body.

In my ecstasy I felt him tense, his whole body became rigid as his climax neared. His right hand moved up my body to my breast, his lips followed. He bit the hard nipple, not enough to break the skin, just right to once again push me over the edge.

I felt his hot semen explode deep inside of me as he too gave in to the climax.

Chapter Thirty-Three

What the fuck was I going to do now?

Gabriel struck a chord with me. He was getting under my skin. Big time.

Even my trysts with Metisse didn't quench my need to jump Gabriel's bones. Gabriel touched me in ways that Metisse didn't. Literally and figuratively, but mainly literally.

Sex with Metisse was intimate, soothing even, though it could get heated. We made love. We never went too far, never crossed the line. Not even in feline form.

With Gabriel it was rough, maybe even violent at times, but oh so satisfying. I was slowly becoming addicted to both of them.

This was definitely not the plan. I had to stop the imminent war, quickly, and clear up the mess I was getting myself into with these two hotties.

I thought I'd figured it out; killing Gabriel would solve the problem and I could continue to have my little trysts with Metisse. But now, now I had really fucked up. I was getting deeper and deeper into this mess. Something had to give. But what?

Even riding through the dark forest on the bike hadn't cleared my mind. The big two-cylinder thundering between my legs usually had a calming effect, but now, even that didn't help.

Revving the gas up I increased the speed to a dangerous level. I threw it into the curves, the exhausts screeching over the ground with every right turn. I didn't care. I needed to get this out of my system. I howled into the night, even over stemming the deep thunder of the Harley. Nothing helped.

I threw the bike into yet another curve, too fast—much too fast. The back wheel slipped and lost its grip on the tarmac. The scream of the metal hurt my ears. I countered and tried to right the bike as I came out onto the straight stretch. The back wheel flipped from one side to the other. It threatened to crash the bike and me with it to the unyielding blacktop. It would hurt; badly. Broken bones, road rash. All of it flashed in my mind as I struggled to keep the bike upright.

I finally managed to regain my balance and let go of the gas while I steered the bike to the side of the road. I kicked out the stand as I killed the engine.

Once the shaking stopped, I got off the bike and walked a few metres into the brush at the roadside. The walking calmed me further and I was finally able to think straight. I got myself into this mess, now I had to get myself out.

OK, it was time to take another look at what I was doing.

I had a mission. I was tasked to stop a war between Werewolves and Sabres. I'd identified who the players were, and in my wisdom thought of a plan that ended in my being romantically involved with both of them.

Hmmm. Not good. At least not if I wanted to keep them both alive. And to tell you the truth, killing either of them would pain me. In my own way I was becoming attached to them.

Both of them.

My thoughts repeatedly came back to Gabriel and Metisse. This was going nowhere.

I needed help. Someone to talk to. Yeah, like this was a conversation I could have with anyone. These were the times I missed my mother most. She would understand. She knew me. If she'd been around, I probably wouldn't be in this mess.

I returned to the bike, straddled it and turned the key in the ignition when a thought struck me. The last time we spoke she made a strange comment. 'When the time is right, go to Waisland. Talk to he keeps watch.' It hadn't meant anything to me at that time, it sounded rather strange, an unfinished sentence. Now it was a lifeline. Somewhere to start. Not that it meant anything to me now either. It was cryptic. "He keeps watch" what the hell did that mean? No idea.

I turned the bike around and headed back to the farm.

Time to hit the Internet. Time for research.

Chapter Thirty-Four

Internet can be your friend and your enemy.

There is such a wealth of information on the web you can educate yourself on anything you want. If you can find it, that is. The sheer volume of data works against you when it's just that one little bit of information you have to work with.

I started off with "Waisland". That was a given, that I combined with "observation" reasoning that someone who watches would probably be in an observation post.

That gave no sensible leads, so I changed "observation" to "investigation", using the thesaurus to find synonyms for the words.

After three hours and multiple cups of coffee, my eyes started to blink profusely with fatigue. This was not my idea of fun. It was leading me nowhere. I tried the regular web and finally the paranormal and dark one.

In desperation, I finally entered "he who watches" and "Montana" in the google search field and was rewarded by another seventeen-and-a-half million hits.

How the hell was I going to find one man in all this data? Then a thought struck me. What if that was his name? "He who watches" it could be a name. Now slightly apprehensive, I typed that in the field with "name" behind it.

OK, that got rid of a million hits. Then I added "Native American" and the number of hits skyrocketed. But I was sure that I was on the right track.

That reinvigorated me.

I grabbed yet another cup of coffee and looked up Native American history in Montana.

The fur over my spine started to prick through the skin as adrenaline flowed through my veins. This felt good. Better than anything I had done in the past hours.

The Native American people had a centuries old strong connection with the paranormal world. I berated myself for not taking them into the equation earlier.

They came to the continent of North America long before we did and made it their home. Then, according to legend, thousands of years ago the Wolves come. Fierce warriors in their long boats. They came ready for war but were welcomed by the spiritual tribes in what is now Newfoundland.

They mingled with the native population and moved consecutively south, carving out their own territories alongside the tribes who lived there. Always living in harmony with nature and the people. All until the conquerors came.

They were the first strong lead I had.

I searched all day and found a lot of information about the tribes who made this place their home. The Blackfoot was the main tribe in the area around Waisland. They'd lived in this area for longer than recorded history. That made them my first port of call. I found a site dedicated to the Blackfoot; from there I looked up Blackfoot names and their meaning and struck gold. Askuwheteau was a traditional Blackfoot boy's name. Its translation was "he keeps watch".

My new challenge was how to approach them. I could hardly drive up to the council house on my bike and demand to speak to the chiefs.

A thought crossed my mind. The pack. Wolves and Native Americans had mingled throughout the centuries of coexistence. The pack members all had what I originally thought were Hispanic characteristics. I realised I'd made a stupid mistake. Their ancestors weren't Hispanic. They were Native American. They would know more. Maybe even help.

Chapter Thirty-Five

Later the next night I lay in Gabriel's arms as he softly stroked my hair. My fingers followed the contours of his chest, lightly passing over the skin and the soft fur that always lingered for a while after our love making.

This was the first time we'd taken our time. Our needs hadn't dictated the pace and it was almost serene. Deep in my being I felt the connection that I tried my best to ignore. Gabriel was a part of me. Whether I liked it or not, we were joined in a way that transcended the physical. I guess you could call it love, but it was much, much more than that. This was a centuries old pull, designed by nature to bring the best characteristics together. The thump of Gabriel's heart soothed me. Pushed the anxiety of the connection to the background for the moment. I would deal with that later. 'When?' That pesky voice at the back of my mind asked. 'When I want to,' I answered silently to shut it up.

Gabriel noticed my agitation. 'Are you okay?' he whispered into my hair.

'Yeah,' I answered unconvincingly.

He laughed. Gabriel was very sensitive to my moods. He read them like a book. He read me like a book. It already caused some quite anxious moments. But that was the thing about Wolves. They observed. They noticed.

'Spill the beans,' he laughed. 'You're going to anyway.'

I pushed my upper body up onto my elbows and looked down at my lover. The amusement made his eyes sparkle. The lines around them gave him character and depth. They softened his visage and made my spine tingle. His black beard with the occasional grey-white hair usually made him look hard and dangerous. Now it appeared soft and welcoming.

In the pack, he was the alpha. The strength of the pack. Never wavering. Dominant. When he was with me, he was a totally different man. His big heart showed. Along with a burning urge to love and be loved. He'd yearned to find his mate for hundreds of years, never making that one connection that completed him, that made him whole. This he found with me.

Regret and sorrow threatened to make me cry out. He was my target. I had to kill him. But here I was, living a connection that even I could not ignore. What the fuck was I going to do? I closed my eyes to frantically push back the tears.

I felt the soft touch of his hand as he pushed my hair away from my face.

'What is it, my love?' he asked softly. 'I can help.'

'No. Not this time,' I answered. 'At least, not yet.' I looked deep into his eyes. 'This I have to do myself.'

I tried to lighten the moment. 'Let's change the subject for now.' He observed me intently, deciding whether to push the question. Thankfully, he just smiled and kissed me.

'OK, what shall we talk about now?'

This was my chance. I pretended to think for a few seconds. 'Where did the pack come from?' I asked.

He took a deep breath, raised an eyebrow and answered me. 'The pack has been here for more than two thousand years. They came from the northeast, from what is now Canada. They settled here and stayed through all the challenges that were thrown against them. It is our home.'

'Was it deserted when the pack arrived?'

'No, there were Native people here, the Blackfoot, Kootenai, Gros Ventre, Crow and many more.'

'What happened?' I asked 'When you arrived. Did you fight for the land?'

'We didn't have to. The Blackfoot welcomed us to their territory. They had an age-old history with the spiritual, and their Shaman was intimately knowledgeable about our kind. I think he had some Wolf blood in him. He came out to a clearing on the mountain top at full moon and waited for the pack. His chanting led them there and they surrounded him. None of them attacked. They waited to see what would happen. I guess they were confused. Humans usually ran from them. Anyway, the alpha pair approached the Shaman, and a truce was made. One that has lasted through thousands of years.'

'You still have a truce?'

'It's not necessary anymore. The tribe and the Wolves intermingle, share their blood and heritage. Most of the pack have Blackfoot blood in them now, and a lot of the tribe have Wolf ties. We are brothers.'

I digested what he told me. The connection I'd deduced was there and much more pronounced than I'd expected. Now what?

'OK, spit it out,' Gabriel broke my reverie. 'Ask what you really want to know.'

'What do you mean?'

He laughed again. 'Cut out the innocent act, Trish, I'm not falling for it. There's something on your mind. Something connected to the pack and the tribe. You might as well ask what it is that's eating you up.'

I smiled. He knew me so well. I would have to be careful. There were still things he could not know. Like my deceit.

'Is there someone in the tribe called Askuwheteau?'

'Yes,' he answered. The crease in his brow deepened. This was a very direct and detailed question, not what he expected. 'He is the Shaman. Why?'

'I need to talk to him,' I answered.

'About what?' Now it was his turn to question me.

'Please, Gabriel. This is something I cannot share completely with you now. Not yet. I need to talk to him. Ask him about something my mother said the day before she died.'

'What was that?'

'She just said, "talk to he who watches." That is Askuwheteau in....'

'In Blackfoot. Yes, I know. What did she mean?'

'I don't know,' I answered truthfully. 'But I need to find out. Could you take me to see him?'

His eyes pierced mine, probing for more information, answers to all the unspoken questions I could see in his face. Please Gabriel, I thought, just go with me on this. Don't look too deep—not now. I don't want to lose you yet.

'OK,' he finally answered. I let out the breath that I didn't know I was holding and smiled.

'Great. Let's do that tomorrow.' My left hand continued to follow the contours of his muscles, only now the nails were more pronounced, sending goosebumps up and down his arms. 'And now, let's do something else.'

My hand moved down further, past the six-pack to the awakened member in the black curls of his pubic hair. I grabbed him and squeezed. He gasped and forgot all about any questions he might have had.

Chapter Thirty-Six

We thundered through the gates of the reservation at two o'clock the next afternoon.

I followed Gabriel down the rough track. You couldn't call it a road. The tarmac stopped just after the sign that announced we were nearing the reservation.

The road wasn't the only sign of poverty here. We rode at a snail's pace through haphazardly placed trailers, broken down trucks and rusty agricultural vehicles. Small children followed our progress with empty eyes. The state of their clothes and occasional shoes was tantamount to the hardships these people faced.

These were the tribes that had been displaced from their ancestral grounds after gold was found there. They were moved time and time again as each site proved to have some value after all for the white Americans. Finally, once all the precious metals had been removed and the soil completely ravished, the people were sent back.

Yet another travesty in American history.

My heart went out to the people here. They had been

relentlessly persecuted. As were we; the paranormal. If you could find us that is. We are amongst you. We hide. But we fight back. Here, I could see no way out. No hope.

Occasionally someone would wave to Gabriel and he would acknowledge them. I just followed in his shadow. Feeling worse very minute.

The dirt track took us past the centre of what was probably the village and out into the barren wilderness. Three miles on, we stopped at a small wooden cabin amid fenced paddocks. Four horses stared at us as we killed the engines and stepped off the bikes. One neighed. A warning? It sounded like it. Maybe they sensed the Wolf in Gabriel, though I had the distinct feeling their nervousness was aimed at me, not him.

Gabriel smiled slightly and nodded his head for me to follow him as he led the way up the two steps to the doorway. He knocked. We waited. I wanted to knock again, get inside, out from the stares of the horses. They unnerved me for some strange reason. In my animal form I hunted horses as well as other prey animals, killed them. But now they gave me goosebumps.

'Come in, Sinpoa.' Finally, a voice from inside.

It occurred to me that the occupant of the house wasn't able to see who was at his door. There was no camera or spy hole in the door. OK, he could have recognised the big-twin, but that could have been anyone from the pack. And who was Sinpoa anyway?

We walked through the door into a surprisingly light and bright interior. Native art and blankets adorned the walls and made a colourful impression. Baskets and pots completed the almost museum quality of the artefacts. It was stunning. I turned around to take in all that was on show here. Yet it was not staged. It was a home. A throwback to another time. History called to me from all sides.

I turned back to face the man sitting in the chair opposite the door. He was completely not what I expected. My imagination had prepared me for an old man, reminiscent of the photos of Sitting Bull that I had seen on Internet; weathered with his long hair in plaits along-side his head. Maybe even with the mandatory feather at the back of his head.

My surprise must have showed. Gabriel chuckled softly. I glanced at him and admonished him with my eyes. He could have told me.

The Shaman didn't look much older than I did, beginning to mid-thirties. His skin was smooth and without wrinkles. The hair on either side of his long face was shorn close to the skull and the bright neon coloured mohawk was almost as surprising as the tribal tattoos on both sides of his face. He was dressed in a polo shirt that didn't even try to hide his physique or his tattoos. This man would have been completely at home in the art district of Los Angeles. Not what I expected in the midst of a depressing Native American reservation in the desolate lands outside of Waisland.

He smiled, breaking the stern visage that greeted me when I walked in. I don't know if that threw me even more.

'I've been waiting for you,' he said. I nodded, not sure whether he was addressing me or Gabriel. 'You took your time.'

He stood up and surprised me yet again. The Shaman stood about eight feet tall. I had to look up to him as he approached me.

OK, so it was me he was waiting for. What the hell did he mean? We just decided we would visit him yesterday.

Gabriel hadn't called in advance, so what was he waiting for? How did he know?

He held out his hand. 'I am Askuwheteau. But you know that don't you? Welcome, Altermichan.'

The hair on my arms stood on end. The resemblance of the Shaman to Cantix got to me. He was tall, he knew my real name. This was getting weird. And dangerous. My first instinct was to turn and run out of the cabin. Fire up the bike and get the hell out of Dodge.

'It's good to see you again,' he continued.

Again? What the fuck?

'I've never seen you before,' I exclaimed, surprised at the defiance in my voice.

He laughed. I glanced at Gabriel; he was just as astounded as I was.

'We met when you were a mere babe. Three months old I believe. Your parents brought you here.' Yeah, right, pull the other one, it's got bells on it. This guy was nuts. My parents? My father and mother were not together when I was born. He left her. At least that was what I deduced from my mother. She never spoke of him directly. I had no real idea of who he was. Just what he was. That I knew.

'Bullshit. You would have been a baby yourself. How would you have remembered?' I spat back.

'As you, I am older than I look. I have been around for hundreds of years. Long enough to see you as an infant.' He was totally calm as he walked into the open kitchen and opened a cupboard under the side cabinet. He pulled out a bottle of what looked like whisky and three glasses which he set down on the table between us. 'Drinks anyone?'

It was early for alcohol, much too early.

Despite that, I nodded. I needed a drink with all that was going on here. It was beyond strange. My instincts still screamed at me to leave. But another voice, one I recognised as my mother, urged me to stay.

Askuwheteau poured generous amounts of whisky into the glasses and stepped back to return to his chair.

He looked comfortable, completely at ease. The very opposite of my demeanour. He sipped his drink and casually observed me.

Gabriel stepped forward, picked up the remaining two glasses and offered me one. I took it, my eyes transfixed on the Shaman. I sniffed the drink, it smelled okay, and downed a large amount in one go. The alcohol burned my throat as it passed on to my stomach. I almost gagged at the reflux when the liquid hit my gut. Man, that was strong stuff.

Again, the chuckle from Askuwheteau.

The Shaman gestured to the seat opposite him. I hesitantly walked the two steps and lowered myself down onto the elk hide in the rattan seat. There was no seat for Gabriel. He glanced around, obviously noticing the same.

'Sinpoa,' Askuwheteau said. 'Would you please wait outside? Altermichan and I have things we need to discuss.' He didn't make it seem like the dismissal that it actually was.

Gabriel's brow creased and he cocked his head in question. The Shaman didn't offer any additional explanation. He just waited for Gabriel to leave. My lover glanced at me, I nodded. He drained the glass and stepped out of the cabin, squeezing my shoulder as he walked past.

I sipped the whisky as we waited for the door to close.

'Sinpoa?' I asked. Easy questions first.

'That's his Blackfoot name,' he explained. 'He is a member of the tribe.'

'He's not full Blackfoot,' I countered, completely on the

defensive. My attitude didn't seem to rile the Shaman. He was just as relaxed as when we arrived.

'No. He isn't.'

'But neither are you.' It wasn't a question. Anyone who has lived as long as he had and still looked early thirties wasn't completely human.

'Again—no. I am not. But that is of no consequence within the tribe. They accept all who are of the same disposition and mind. Ours is a tribe of like-minded. The body is just a detail.'

'Even if they are Werewolves?'

'Even if they are Werewolves,' he confirmed.

'I don't know what you think you know about me?' I continued. 'But I have never met you before and I'm not falling for your bullshit.'

He seemed unperturbed by my aggressive attitude.

'Who sent you here?' he asked softly.

That hurt. He went right for the jugular. 'My mother,' I whispered.

'And do you trust her?' There was no malice in his words, just clarity.

'Yes.' My answer was barely audible.

'That is why you are here,' he continued. 'You need answers to questions you do not dare speak out loud.'

He was reading my mind. He had to be. That, or I was really more of an open book than I thought.

'Your parents were fearful for you. They were aware of the prophecy and the implications it had for you.'

'What prophecy?' I whispered, taking another sip. The burning was reassuring. It meant that I was awake and that this was not a dream.

'There is an ancient Oglala Sioux prophecy; "Darkness will descend over the tribes. The world will be out of balance. Floods, forest and earthquakes will ensue. A White Buffalo Calf Woman will purify the world. She will bring back harmony and spiritual balance."'

He let that sink in. I couldn't fathom what he meant. What White Buffalo Calf woman? I shrugged in frustration.

'The prophecy has been interpreted in many different ways throughout the history of the Native American tribes,' Askuwheteau explained. 'One of the explanations refers to the paranormal community. The darkness is symbolical for the Council, their rule is one of darkness and violence. They kill anything that stands in their way, all to consolidate the power they have over their paranormal brethren. The Council uses the age-old divide-and-conquer tactics, pitting the factions against each other. That way they can steer the world in the way they want.'

His words resounded with me. The Council sent me to Waisland to kill the leaders of the two largest paranormal groups in the USA. What had Cantix said?

'My mission is to make sure that there are no more thoughts of rebellion and war.' I repeated his words out loud. The Shaman nodded. The nagging feeling I experienced ever since my meeting with Cantix was finally becoming concrete. The mist was lifting.

'There is no imminent war between the Wolves and the Sabres,' I stated. 'He sent me here to stop them from amassing too much power. They are a threat to him and to the Council.' My anger fuelled my understanding.

Red clouded my vision. I was being used. Used, to keep the Council in power and consolidate their killing grip on those I loved. I didn't even question how the Shaman apparently knew about my mission, or why he seemed unperturbed by the knowledge.

'The Oracle never saw a war.' My tone and volume mirrored my anger.

'She did,' Askuwheteau answered to my surprise. 'She predicted an all-out war. Only not between the Wolves and the Sabres. There will be a war against the Council.'

It was all beginning to fall into place.

'And what is my role in all this?' I asked. 'Why did my mother send me to you?' I knew the answer.

'Remember the White Buffalo Calf Woman?' he said. I nodded. 'Don't take that literally. It's a metaphor for someone who will lead the people against the oppressors.'

'And you think that is me?'

'The White Buffalo Calf Woman is one of two worlds. Like you.'

We spoke for another hour.

The final pieces of the puzzle fell neatly into place. The prophecy, and everything that happened to me since I took this mission, was cryptic. I'd been in the dark from day one. Unexpected and mysterious twists faced me every step I took. It had frustrated me, the inconsistency, the emotions, everything.

Now it all made complete sense.

Chapter Thirty-Seven

I walked out the door into the sunlight. Gabriel sat on the steps throwing pebbles. He refused to look at me. His visage was full of resentment—I suppose because he was sent outside while I spoke with the Shaman. He was the alpha. He answered to no one, and now he had been sent packing like a lowly omega. That did not go down well with him. The only things that stopped him from barging in on us were his love for me and respect for Askuwheteau. It took a lot out of him. He was fuming. Yeah, well tough. There were more important things going on here than his wounded ego.

That wasn't fair, and I knew it. He was governed by the wolf hierarchy and instincts. He had no say in this. It was in his genes. Plain and simple. I admired him for the way he tried to restrain his anger, and how he conceded to the Shaman.

I placed my hand on his arm, felt the tension in the muscles beneath the leather jacket. He raised his head just enough to look me in the eye. I could see the struggle there.

Instinct against love. Against respect for me, for the Shaman.

I smiled slightly, squeezed his arm and softened my own eyes. It worked. The muscles relaxed a little and the creases in his brow softened.

Askuwheteau stood in the doorway. 'Thank you Sinpoa.' He acknowledged the battle raging inside the Alpha. 'I know that was not easy for you. It was, however, necessary. This was between her and me. Altermichan will let you know, when the time is right. Trust her. She will do what is best.'

That struck a chord with me. Just a few hours ago I was planning on killing Gabriel. I was sure the Shaman knew this. He knew much more even than he had told me. The man who looked like a thirty-year old was ancient and possessed the wisdom of his long years. He would be a worthy opponent to Aquanaris.

Now that was thought.

And he trusted me to do the right thing. No pressure.

I wondered whether he knew about Metisse. He must do. How? I didn't know.

My opinion of oracles did a one-eighty. There were genuine people who could see the future, or what the future could be. This guy was legit. He'd convinced me. Given me insight.

And that made me all the more dangerous.

I nodded to the Shaman and turned to the bikes. I needed some time to digest all he told me and the conclusions I'd made myself.

I had to formulate a new plan.

One with a different outcome.

Chapter Thirty-Eight

Gabriel calmed down a bit by the time we made it back to town. He stopped outside the Fifties Diner. I'd forgotten the time, and my stomach reminded me it was way past dinner time. Gabriel obviously had the same idea. We parked the bikes outside the gaudy building that mirrored a massive aluminium Airstream caravan and took the two steps up from the sandy driveway to the electric door of the diner. It whooshed open and invited us into the air-conditioned restaurant. Black and white tiles on the floor and Formica booths with bright red plastic benches lined the windowed side of the building screamed the fifties. Opposite them was a long chrome bar with round stools that stood on single columns of chrome. Most were in use. Buddy Holly chimed from the original Wurlitzer Jukebox in the corner. The waitresses were young, blonde and dressed in fifties garb. It was very cliché, but the food was good.

Franny, the owner, welcomed us and waved us towards an empty booth. Gabriel kissed her on the cheek and sat down. I took the seat opposite him. I wanted to see his face and gauge the impact the meeting with Askuwheteau had on him, especially the last part.

Franny brought two bottles of beer and placed them in front of us. 'The usual?' she asked.

'Yes please.' Gabriel was all smiles. She looked at me. I nodded. We came here enough for her to know what we liked. She left us to place our order with the two cooks who kept food flowing from the kitchen to the ever-present customers.

'You going to say anything?' I asked Gabriel.

He looked up from the table he was studying intensely.

'What's there to say?' he answered my question with one of his own. So, it's like that? Well, good with me. If he wanted to sulk, then be my guest. I thought he was above that.

'Nothing I guess,' I shrugged. If he wanted to play the silence game, then that's what we would do. I was good at it. Years of practice had made me patient. You needed that in my line of work. If you wanted to stay alive.

Franny brought our dinner. The scent of one-hundred-percent beef hamburgers with freshly baked bread preceded her and we both turned in anticipation of the fantastic tastes. She put the heavily laden plates in front of us, tasted the tension between us and left without her usual happy banter.

We ate in silence.

Finally, Gabriel pushed his empty plate away and turned his face up towards me. 'Did you get what you came for?' he asked. The edge was only a memory. The food, and probably the silence, had mellowed him.

'Yes,' I answered, equally friendly. 'And no.' I finished the last bite of my hamburger and wiped my fingers on the paper serviette. 'I don't really know what I expected. Definitely not that he knew me. Or what he thinks that I am. It feels like I have even more questions now.'

His face was once again soft and loving. I leaned over and took his hand. As I stroked my fingers over his hard knuckles, I understood what it had cost Gabriel to go outside and not be part of what the Shaman and I shared. 'I'm sorry you could not be part of it all,' I said sincerely.

'Askuwheteau has his reasons,' he answered. He obviously held the strange Shaman in high regard.

'I hope so.' I continued to hold his hand. Slowly he responded, his fingers closing over mine. He leant forward, towards me. The warmth and tingles once again prevailing between us. I let the nails on my fingers elongate and the soft stroking took on a new dimension. His eyes lit up and I could see my ministrations were having the desired effect.

'Let's get out of here,' he said huskily.

'Now you're talking,' I answered in a seductive voice that immediately impacted. I stood up from the booth and walked quickly to the door, he caught up and grabbed my butt. Never one for subtlety, he staked his claim. Our laughter followed us out the door as Gabriel called back to Franny. 'Put it on my tab, Fran.'

'Sure thing, sweetness,' we heard as I opened the door and almost fell through. 'Have fun.'

'Don't worry. We will,' I wanted to call back. But it was totally redundant.

Chapter Thirty-Nine

The pack easily accepted me.

As the imprinted mate of the Alpha, I was immediately one of them. There was no jealousy here. No anger at him bringing in someone who was obviously not a full-blooded Werewolf. What I actually was, they didn't know, but it made no difference. Gabriel staked his claim and that was good enough for them.

I felt at home in the pack. A strange feeling for someone who had essentially been alone from childhood. I'd always fended for myself and the feeling of togetherness resounding from the pack was soothing and new. It struck a chord within me I never knew I had.

The disadvantage of this feeling was that I started to feel lonely when I wasn't around the pack. Not of course when I was with Metisse. He made me feel wanted and loved, as did Gabriel.

But the clan was completely different from the pack. There, people were more outspoken. Less inclined to accept what the clan leader said without an explanation. I had friends there, but also enemies.

In the pack, there was no reluctance to accept me. I think the pack was closer to my own disposition. The pomp and status of the clan's jet-set life was lost on me. The pack was just plain and simple family.

I divided my time between my two lovers and tried to make sense of what was happening to me.

Alex pestered me continuously for more information about when I would finally fulfil my mission. He was approaching a very dangerous stage with me. He always got on my nerves, but more and more I found myself imagining strange and painful ways I would employ to shut him up. His constant complaints and bickering were driving me mad.

My patience waned quickly. Not just towards Alex—though mainly there—but towards everyone. I knew it wasn't really personal. It was all due to my loss of control.

Ever since I was thrown head-on into a solitary life, my very existence depended on me. I was the only one I could count on.

In the early years, before I learned the price of trust, there was a close call when I was almost kidnapped and sold into slavery. It taught me never to trust anyone. No matter who they were or how many other people vouched for them. I controlled what happened to me. No one else.

Even my time as an Assassin for the Council was a calculated step in my goal to avenge my mother. A slight loss of control there would mean my death. If they found out… Well, it wouldn't end well. That was for sure.

My visit to the Shaman opened up a can of worms.

What the fuck was going on here? Was he the one my mother had been talking about? He had to be. There were too many coincidences. He knew me. Or at least knew of me. He hinted at things I had never told anyone.

Then he started to talk nonsense. That stupid prophecy. I didn't really believe people could predict the future with any real measure of certainty any more than I could. Sure, there were things that were obvious, everyone with half a brain could add two and two together and come up with something close to four.

I always believed oracles and seers were charlatans. All of them, with the queen-bitch Aquanaris heading off the line.

Askuwheteau struck me as surprisingly genuine. What he said struck a nerve. Where did that leave me? It was completely frustrating. I didn't know what to believe. All of this. The whole mission. Both of my lovers. They were distractions I didn't need right now.

Even the peace I felt with the pack wasn't enough to calm my frayed nerves. I found myself snapping at people. Gabriel tried to sooth me; he must have realised my change in demeanour was the result of the visit to the Shaman.

'Are you OK, Trish?' he finally asked as I downed yet another bottle of beer. I wasn't even tasting it. It just flowed down my throat in an attempt to quench a thirst that had nothing to do with liquids.

I bit back my retort. He was just concerned. There was no reason to bite his head off. 'Yeah,' I replied attempting a smile. I wasn't kidding him; he saw through it.

'Why don't you go back to the Shaman?' Was he reading my mind? 'Maybe he can answer whatever it is that's eating you up.' He knew me so well.

'He'll just cause more questions,' I countered.

Gabriel took my hand and squeezed it in support. There wasn't much more that he could do.

I was being a consummate bitch, and I knew it. But there was nothing I could do about it. I was so frustrated with myself I was taking it out on everyone close. Here they just accepted it and took the brunt of my bad moods.

I avoided Metisse and the clan after the last visit when I almost bit his head off. It was counterproductive. But I couldn't help it.

The next beer didn't help. Neither did the one after that.

It was going to be a long night.

Chapter Forty

As the sun set over the mountains, I left Gabriel in anger. We fought. I don't really know what about. My nerves were shredded. My moods dark and dangerous. I was not easy to be around. It hurt Gabriel. I know. I could see it in his eyes, in his stance. He tried to make me happy. Everything I asked for he did, as long as it didn't interfere with his status as the alpha. But nothing was enough for me. I needed him. Wanted him. But I pushed him away at the same time. He was becoming as frustrated as I was. I hardly recognised myself anymore.

I rode the bike all night. Not heading to any specific destination. Just riding. Trying to get the wind to blow the anger out of my head. It didn't work. Nothing did.

I felt really bad. A failure. My one goal in life—vengeance for my mother—was slipping away from me. The mission that should have been just a sidestep was starting to engulf me. And not in the way it should.

The need I experienced now was new for me. Proud of

my self-control all my life, this feeling of disorientation terrified me. My control was what brought me through the period after I lost my mother; the only family that I ever knew.

I felt abandoned. Then my anger transformed to survival. No more than a child, life on my own was hard, vicious even.

The Council hadn't found what they were looking for when they killed Mum. They searched for me for many years. Thankfully, they had no idea what I looked like. I moved constantly, living off what I could steal. I slept in forests, in caves, in dilapidated abandoned barns.

Mum had home-schooled me to read and write. I was a voracious reader and continued to devour any books I could get my hands on. I educated myself in more ways than one. Savvy to the ways of the underworld and armed with the knowledge of the books and later the Internet, I survived.

Slowly I found a place in the world. The tough life made me hard. I learned how to kill. First, those who hunted me, later those I thought deserved to die. My prowess increased and with that my status in the paranormal underworld.

All that time I was consumed with the obsession to gain vengeance for my mother. I pushed any feelings or emotions to the back of my mind and locked them away. I had no use for them. Only anger and brutality. Those I nurtured.

I made a name for myself and gained contracts that allowed me to live in more opulence. I became wealthy, though I hid it away. In my line of work, secrecy was a survival necessity.

Just when I was at odds on how to get closer to my ultimate targets, fate intervened. My reputation preceded me. Cantix, then on his way up in the Council, heard of me and saw the potential for another paranormal assassin.

The paranormal world is, out of necessity, one that is strongly regulated. It is a secret world, and its existence depends on staying just that—concealed.

Humans think they rule the world. We leave them in that delusion. They are small-minded and would not be able to get their little brains around what lived around them. The paranormal has infiltrated all levels of human society, and we pull the strings. The few of our kind that exposed themselves to humans over the centuries paid the ultimate price. The witch hunts. Inquisitions. All the result of clashes between humans and us.

As a result, we stay in the shadows. Became the stuff of myths and later, horror films. Humans relegate werewolves and wizards to the realms of fantasy.

They have no idea.

My first encounter with Cantix had been a difficult one. It strained even my nerves. He sent a group of wizards to pick me up. I killed two of them before they managed to fabricate some kind of kinetic energy cage around me. With the assistance of an ogre, they moved the cage to the Council's grand hall. I was unceremoniously dumped in front of the horseshoe table, while the wizards licked their wounds.

Cantix was the only Council member present. He observed the wizards with open disdain. The lead mage stumbled up to the platform but was ushered away with a wave of Cantix's hand. The dismissal was clear.

Cantix stood up and approached the kinetic cage. I stayed put and observed the man as he did me. I had never seen anyone that tall up close.

Sure, I knew what he looked like. Everyone in the paranormal world did. He was legendary. Up close he was much more impressive. His gilded cloak emphasised the size of the man, giving the illusion that he was even taller than the ten feet he was. He moved with long strides, easily spanning the distance to the cage with five steps where I would have needed at least twenty.

He walked around the bubble. I stayed put. I flatly refused to show any nerves or follow his movements. He was just another bully. I bowed to no one.

He finished his circling and stood in front of me.

'Release her,' he ordered. The wizards looked at each other in shock, then at the lead mage. He nodded and they broke their spells, moving backwards as they did, just to be sure that they were out of range of my double-bladed knives.

'Welcome, Altermichan.' Cantix was completely at ease. 'I asked the wizards to invite you here,' he continued.

'Yeah,' I answered, 'I declined.'

Cantix laughed. A deep rumble without any mirth.

He was cold. Dangerous. Well so was I.

'Obviously,' he said, observing the wounded wizards. 'Join me in a drink.'

It wasn't really a request, more of an order. I let that one pass and followed him up to the table. Cantix took his place on the gigantic throne and a chair was brought to the opposite side of the table for me. I sat.

Crystal cut glasses filled with wine were set in front of us. I waited until Cantix took a first sip of his before I took a glass. I sniffed the sweet liquor. Too sweet, not exactly my taste, but now was not the time to be picky. Not with him.

'You have quite a reputation.' He was finally getting down to the reason for all of this. I stayed silent.

'How would you like to continue your vocation in the service of the Council?'

As if I had any choice. I was acutely aware of the fact that saying "no" would be a death sentence. The wizards who brought me here were of a completely different order than Cantix. I wouldn't get out of here alive if he didn't want me to.

On the other hand, for the past two years I had been racking my brains how to get into the inner circle of the Council. This offer was just too good to pass up. I would work for them, sure. But that was only temporary. Until I found the information I was searching for. Then, after exacting my revenge, I would disappear. Or die, whichever came first.

'You have exceptional abilities,' he continued. 'You are a shapeshifter?'

It was barely a question. I just nodded. It benefitted me to have the Council think I was a shapeshifter. They hold a higher status than the lowly creatures that can only shift into one form other than human.

Shapeshifters can take on any form they want. This makes them highly versatile and able to infiltrate any paranormal environment. What I really was had to remain a secret, at any cost. It would make me the hunted instead of the hunter.

'You will answer to the Council, and to me.'

Yeah, to him then. The Council part was just for anyone listening in. Who's he kidding? Not me.

'I will supply you with a target, and you will take care of the wet work for me.'

'Paranormals?' I dared to ask.

'Anyone that needs to disappear.'

OK, so that includes humans. That was new for me. I'd only taken on contracts for my own kind up to now. A reaction from my side wasn't called for, so I left it at that.

'I have a first contract for you.' He pushed an envelope towards me. The fat beige container was a disappointment.

The entourage we were in called for a parchment or something ancient and dramatic, not just a simple brown paper envelope you could buy in any supermarket.

I was becoming cynical again. Time to reign that in. Not the right time, or the right place. But hey, that's me.

I left the envelope where it was and continued to sip my wine.

'I trust we have an agreement,' Cantix said. I couldn't remember that we'd actually discussed anything about my new job, or the salary for that matter. But in his world, all was clear.

OK, I'd run with that. See where it brought me. I wasn't in this for the money anyway. I had enough of that. More than a hundred years of contracts have given me a nice fortune.

I nodded.

'Good,' he said as he stood up to leave.

I remained seated. That resulted in a collective gasp from the wizards and a smile from Cantix. He understood my defiance and let this one pass. I couldn't do it again. I knew that. But I had to make my own statement. With a last gaze at me, he turned and left the hall.

I sat in the chair and sipped at the nauseatingly sweet wine. God, how can anyone drink this shit?

I put the half full glass down on the table, picked up the envelope and made my way out of the hall with a last 'see ya, guys. It was fun,' towards the cowering wizards.

Since then, I've taken care of the Council's dirty work. I wasn't the only one; there are more assassins.

The power of the Council isn't accepted everywhere or by all paranormal creatures. We are called upon to bring the recalcitrant ones back under the Council's umbrella. Or whip as I call it. The past year and a half I handled thirteen assassinations. Not a massive amount, but more than enough to gain their trust.

And here I was in Waisland. On one of the biggest missions they had given me, and I was making a mess of it.

No worse; I was making a mess of me.

Chapter Forty-One

'The owl, that was you?' I asked Askuwheteau.

'Yes,' he answered, closely examining my reactions. I had no way to process all the things going on inside my head. Desperate for at least some answers, I'd drifted back to the Shaman.

I was alone this time.

The sound of my bike was muted in the dark hours of the night as I passed through the gates of the reservation.

No one was out. A single dog barked in the distance but was silenced by its owner's shout. No lights were on. It was even more desolate than in daytime, something I thought would be impossible.

I drove through the village at a snail's pace, only opening the engine up after I had left the slumbering inhabitants.

The short drive from there to Askuwheteau's cabin was over in minutes. I approached the cabin carefully. Slowly.

There were lights on in the building. The horses that stared at me the first time I was there came out of the open barn to investigate.

Again, one horse let out a neigh. A warning. For a moment there I thought I saw a red glow in its eyes. Was it more than it looked? Probably. Anything was possible here.

I killed the engine, kicked out the stand and dismounted the bike. Closely watched by the horses, I made my way up to the door. I hesitated. Why the hell was I here? I berated myself for my foolishness. Just as I was about to turn and walk back to the bike, Askuwheteau's voice broke through the silence.

'Come in, Altermichan. You are welcome.'

Right, well, fuck. Now I couldn't run anymore. He knew it was me.

Of course, he did.

I opened the door and walked in.

The big man was in the same seat as when I saw him last time, once again sipping a drink. It made me wonder whether this was his usual pose; what he did all day long.

I stood in front of him, just inside the door. Fidgeting. My hands wouldn't stay still. I finally crossed my arms in an attempt to calm down.

He smiled. It was a warm smile, one that soothed me a bit. I looked up from his smile to his eyes and lost myself in them. They were a kaleidoscope of colours. Yellows, reds, blues. All at the same time, but not. The shades shifted constantly in the light of the candles and few lamps that were lit. I couldn't remember this from the first visit and was completely mesmerised.

The tension in my shoulders eased up. The knotted muscles relaxed. A warmth filled my body, starting from the pit of my stomach and radiating upwards towards my heart and my brain. On the way it burned away any stress it encountered and left me feeling blissful and completely at ease. Pressure that had built up in the past weeks flowed out of my body effortlessly. Leaving a peace behind I doubted I'd ever experienced before.

Askuwheteau blinked and released me from the connection.

My brow lifted as I opened and closed my own eyes in an attempt to make sense of what just happened. My hands moved of their own accord to my face and I rubbed my eyes. I felt the wet tears on my cheeks and realised that I had been crying. I had been totally unaware of the tears that streamed down my face.

Normally I would have berated myself for such needless emotions. Now it was okay. In a weird and wonderful way, it was good. Maybe relaxing my self-control every now and then had some merit after all.

'You knew I'd be back.' It wasn't a question. He nodded. 'Well, here I am. Now what?' I really had no clue.

'Whatever you want,' he answered.

Oh great. Fat help that was. He indicated a chair behind me, and I sat down. The Shaman poured a large quantity of whisky from the bottle next to him into a second glass that just happened to be on the same table. Coincidence? No. He was expecting me.

I accepted the glass and brought it to my lips. The deep liquid burned a trail down my throat. In a strange way it comforted me. Made me feel alive.

'You know all about what is happening. Don't you?' I finally asked once the burn had receded. He nodded again as he sipped his own drink.

'About Metisse?' Another nod.

'The Council? My mission?' Again.

OK, I'd have to process that.

'What else do you know?'

'I know that you will do the right thing.'

'And what is that?'

Askuwheteau laughed. 'Sorry, no short cuts. You have to figure that out for yourself.'

I hadn't come here for that. 'Why? Why can't you help me? You seem to know everything.' There was an edge to my voice.

He became serious. 'I don't know everything. No one person does. You are going to play a pivotal part in what is to come. But for that it must be completely your own choice. I cannot tell you what to do or influence your way from here.'

'Great!' I threw up my hands. 'What the hell use are you then?'

He didn't react to my ranting. I was pissed off. Mad as hell. I felt manipulated with every turn I made. Mainly by the Council, but not only by them. At least Cantix was clear about his motives. No, scratch that. He was bullshitting me too. And now this. Now the Shaman, who obviously knew a lot more than he disclosed, refused to help me. Throw the mysterious meeting with Charmaine in the mix and it was a recipe for frustration.

'I won't tell you what to do, but I may be able to help you clarify some things. Give you a bit more foundation for your choice,' Askuwheteau added, just when I was about to throw in the towel.

I let that stew for a while and stalled by taking another sip of the whisky. I don't usually drink the stuff, but it was a welcome distraction now.

'OK, Askuwheteau,' I started.

'Call me Ash. It's less of a mouthful.' I was thankful for

that. It had taken a lot of practice to get my tongue around his name. What was it with the Paranormal society that we needed to have unpronounceable and impractical names? Thank God for abbreviations.

'Right, Ash. Let's start with a bit more information about you.' He lifted his brow in surprise. 'You were the owl, and later the heron at the Country Club.' That last one was a guess, but it registered, so I took it as a yes. 'Are you a Shapeshifter?'

He shook his head. 'No. I'm not. You're partially right, I was them, but I'm not the creature itself. I borrow its consciousness. Take it for a ride as it were.'

'You borrow it?' I'd never heard of that before.

'Yes. I hitch a ride in their minds and see through their eyes, hear through their ears.'

'And what happens to them? Afterwards?'

'Nothing. They might be a little bit confused because they have no memory of coming to wherever I took them. But that's all. As is said I "borrow" their consciousness. No harm comes to them.'

'Can you do that with people too?'

'I can.' He was candid, I'll give him that. 'Though not with everyone, there are those who can block me. Others are much easier to connect to.'

'Me?'

'You block me. I don't think that you do it consciously— you already did it as a baby, I cannot connect with your mind.'

Well, that made me feel slightly better. Not that it made much difference. He seemed to know more about me than I did. For a control freak like me, that's bad.

'As a baby?' He referred to seeing me as a baby before.

It just seemed so strange. Mum would have told me. Should have told me.

'Yes. I tried to contact your mind when your parents came here to see me after you were born, but as young as you were, your guards were already up. I think that was one of the things that worried your mother most. That you were so adept at something that most adults don't even get right. She was very worried for you. For your safety.'

'Why?' I knew the answer, but I wanted to hear if he did.

'Because of whom you are.'

'What I am, you mean.'

'Who and what you are is undeniably linked. But I meant who.' His voice softened.

I could feel soft pinpricks behind my eyes. I blinked in an attempt to push away any stupid superfluous emotions I felt. Life had toughened me up. It had bitten me, swallowed me and spat me out. I didn't do emotions. At least, not usually.

This guy was seriously getting to me. Him, and the whole messed up situation I was in now. I prided myself in having my life in order. In being the owner of my destiny. Yeah, right.

'This cannot be easy for you Trish,' he continued in a friendly tone. 'You have been running your whole life because of your destiny. Because of whom you are. Your parents were taken from you and you have been alone for much too long. You don't have to be.'

I thought he just said he couldn't get into my head. It sounded as though he was repeating verbatim everything my stupid emotions were telling me.

'You don't have to run anymore. You can take a stand. We will stand with you. All of us.'

'Take a stand against whom?' My voice broke. I heard a snick and was disgusted with myself. I roughly rubbed the tears from my cheek with my sleeve. This wasn't me. I don't do emotions.

'You know.' There he was again with the cryptic stuff, just when I thought he was starting to help.

I stayed silent. I knew, he'd said. Did I? Did I really? Doubts surfaced, About me, my strength. Everything I had done up to this point. I didn't know my real enemy. Other than the one who was responsible for my mother's death, I had no idea. I tried to push myself farther back in the chair. Escape from all this.

'Stop it,' the voice in the back of my mind shouted without sound. It's an extremely irritating voice, it questions everything and worse than that, it's usually right. OK, so instead of bumming me, how about helping me, I thought. Who is the enemy? Who wants to hurt me, has hurt me in the past? It all boils down to one entity. Everything comes back to that one opponent.

'The Council.' It was barely a whisper.

I looked up at Ash. He nodded slightly, encouraging me to continue.

'Everything comes back to the Council. I was looking for the one person who was responsible for my mother's death, but it's not one. It's the whole. The Council is accountable.'

The familiar heat of rage took root in my abdomen. It felt like a fire I couldn't quench. It heated my blood. Pushed my anger through my veins and into my whole body.

The Council. I pushed my hands on the arm rests of the seat to jump up. I had to do something, get to those responsible. Kill someone. Then common sense brought me back down to earth.

'How the fuck am I supposed to take on the whole Council?'

'Not alone. And not right at this minute.' There was humour in his voice. It was somewhere between laughter and a little bit patronising. I didn't appreciate the last. 'Think it through. You need allies. Many of them. And you have already started to amass your army.'

I looked up. My army? That sounded outright ridiculous. Sure, I'd need one if I was to take on the might of the Council.

'You are not the only one who has a beef with the Council,' Ash continued. 'There is much bad blood towards them. They have killed and persecuted. It is time they paid the price.' That sounded downright revolutionary.

'The Sabres.' I understood what he was saying. They suffered by the hands of the Council. Charmaine still did, every day.

'Amongst others, yes. And you are already aligning yourself with them.'

'Yes, but what about Gabriel and the Wolves?'

'They are also your allies.'

'How can that be? They and the Sabres are sworn enemies. They will not work together.'

'You have ties with both factions. Ties and claims to their loyalty.' He was referring to the bonds of the soul mates. Both Metisse and Gabriel had legitimate claims to me as a mate, and I to them. I felt the pull of both of them. Not as deeply as they did, but there was unmistakably a bond.

'How can I choose?' I asked exasperated.

'Why would you?'

I was flabbergasted. 'Why would I?'

Now that was a novel thought. Why would I indeed?

Food for thought.

Chapter Forty-Two

I spent the next few days alternating between my two lovers and Ash.

First, I went on a road trip with the pack, then to yet another party with Metisse and finally I found myself back in the cabin on the reservation. I had to make a plan and the one person who could help me was Ash.

He wouldn't decide for me—he made that abundantly clear. But I could run my ideas by him. His long life on this planet meant he'd amassed an enormous amount of knowledge. Though very humble about it, the man was a fountain of information. I started to wonder how I made it this far in life without him.

The more we spoke, the better I started to feel about the whole thing. Prophecy and all.

The basis of our plan was to unite the Sabres, the Wolves, and all the other paranormal creatures in the struggle to overthrow the Council. They all had to work together. That meant any old adversity and prejudice would have to make way for cooperation.

There were major challenges. My relationships being the foremost one on my mind. The liaisons gave me a unique insight into the two groups, but they could also be the catalyst for a lot of complications. Neither of the men seemed to me to be the kind who would take quickly to the idea of sharing me. Both were possessive. Both professed they had waited for me for a long time. It was a hurdle that I would have to take. I wasn't looking forward to it.

I tried to get help from Ash, but he could offer no real suggestions. My predicament was new for him too. He just advised me to follow my heart and my intuition where my lovers were concerned. Great. That was what got me in this mess to begin with.

The Sabres and the Wolves would need to get along. Ash didn't seem to think it would be such an issue. That surprised me, but he wouldn't clarify his remark. 'They have more in common than you think,' was all I got out of him.

Once we had these two groups united—and I still thought it was a stretch—we would need to expand our influence. Not just to the other packs and clans, but over the whole paranormal community. How we would achieve this phenomenal task, was our next decision.

We determined that staying in the shadows would not be an option. Once the Council heard of my new mission and finally recognised who I really was, they would throw everything they had at us. It made sense to take the initiative and decide when and where they found out.

This was where my little parasite would come in. I never thought he would actually be of use to me. It would more than likely cost him his life, but that was an occupational hazard in his line of work. Spies never lived long.

Before then, however, we had a lot of work to do. Ash volunteered to contact other paranormals connected to the

Native American people. The original peoples of this country were much more open-minded than the current leaders and had a long history of working and living with paranormals. They also appreciated secrecy.

Ash never ceased to surprise me with the extent of his network. I guess if you've been around for longer than anyone else, you make contacts. He was a fantastic asset to the cause.

Ash refused to talk about himself any more than what he had already shared. 'When the time comes,' was his standard reply to my questions.

I ran into a wall with the prophecy. I knew the basics, and where I fit in. But as with any prophecy it came down to interpretation. Mine was still a bit cloudy. Ash was adamant I was the one meant by "of two worlds" and how that would be an asset. But I was less convinced. It didn't seem that what I was, would be enough to unite the paranormal world in a struggle against the most powerful wizard that had ever existed.

'Don't be so sure,' Ash commented when I voiced my concerns.

'What do you mean?'

'Cantix and Aquanaris are powerful. Without doubt. But theirs' is a control based on fear and terror. It will only prevail until someone breaks the circle. There are other powers that are much stronger and will bring the people together in a common goal; the alleviation of subjugation.'

I looked at him quizzically. 'You're saying there is someone more powerful than him?'

'As I said. It is not the amount of power. It is how you use it that counts.'

Hmm, that was basically a yes. I wondered who he meant. It wasn't me; I knew that. I'm not a wizard. Sure,

I'm strong and very good at what I do, but that alone would not let me get within striking distance of Cantix. I could not hope to kill him myself. The same applied to both of my lovers. So, who would do the deed? I looked at Ash, but he gave no more hints.

I didn't know what he himself was. I didn't think he was a mage, though he showed certain talents that bordered on what I knew some of the wizards possessed. His were more rooted in Native American tradition, much more attuned to nature than to magic. I didn't know if he was a serious contender to oppose Cantix, or Aquanaris for that matter, in an open battle. And he wouldn't enlighten me anymore. He just observed me with a smile in his eyes.

'You will know when the time is right.' Great. Thanks. That was a help.

We both agreed the first thing to do was unite the Sabres and the Wolves. For that we would have to get them to talk, or actually, to listen. It was up to me to get my lovers to come together and listen to what I had to say.

They would need some hefty convincing. Ash promised to be there to support me. I was grateful for that, though I doubted that his presence would have any influence on Metisse. Gabriel looked up to Ash. He respected him. But Metisse? He had no reason to. I didn't even think that he knew who Ash was. Not that I really did, come to think of it. Though I knew that I could trust him. Why? I had no idea. I just did.

'Location is everything,' Ash suggested. 'The clearing where the first treaty was negotiated is the best place to have the meeting. It is neutral terrain, situated on the border of the two territories. The atmosphere of the place will help you convince them to listen to you. Both parties know of the significance of the site. It will not be lost on them. There are

172

spirits there that will sway them. Both the Wolves and the Sabres have longstanding ties to the location where their status quo was determined.'

It made sense. I doubted the sprit thing, but hey, I'm not so easily swayed by what I can't see. I nodded my agreement. The clearing it was.

As I rode the bike back to my safe house, I revisited the decisions we made today. It was all coming down to the wire. I had to do something. The Council would not wait on results forever. If I failed to fulfil their directive, they would send others; assassins who had no emotional involvement. Who would not hesitate to kill both Gabriel and Metisse. I could not let that happen.

The clock was ticking.

Chapter Forty-Three

We received word the Council had summoned us. Me and Alex. Naturally I declined.

'You cannot refuse again.' He tried to sound confident and as usual failed miserably. 'Cantix summoned us to give a report on the mission.'

'I thought you were keeping them informed,' I retorted.

He was so easy to confuse.

'How can I report what I don't know.' He threw up his arms in desperation. 'You never tell me anything.'

OK, that was true, but I wasn't about to agree with him. Going to the Council now would be the worst idea ever. All I learned in the past weeks convinced me of where my true enemies lay, and they were not in Waisland. I couldn't risk losing control when I saw Aquanaris and Cantix again. There was no way I would give them even a chance to find out what I was actually doing. They would play a central position in my plans. But not just yet. There was too much to do before I was ready.

'You go,' I suggested ignoring his earlier comments.

Chapter Forty-Four

We spent the day with Charmaine in the cabin where she regaled me with stories of Metisse's childhood, his somewhat rebellious puberty and the antics he and his friends got themselves into growing up in the Sabre clan. I loved every laugh and every blush that coloured Metisse's handsome face when his mother remembered yet another embarrassing moment she determined just had to be shared.

'Mom!' he exclaimed more than once.

'Oh, come on Metisse. Don't be so heavy handed. Trish is your mate. She needs to know all the things that made you the man you are today.' She waved away his objections. Once Charmaine was on the roll, there was no stopping her.

Later on, the stories took on a much darker character when she spoke about the exile from Canada and how the clan left everything they had behind.

'It was very difficult for our people,' she said. Metisse stood behind his mother, his hand on her shoulder in support. 'Most of us were born in Canada. We lived there our entire lives. Our friends were there. Our very roots.' Her voice was still strong, defiant even. I admired her for her strength and tenacity. This woman was a force to be reckoned with.

'We moved around for almost ten months before we found Waisland,' she continued. 'It was ideal for our purposes. Far away from most of humanity and in a dark spot where we thought the Council couldn't find us.'

'You must understand the Council didn't have the resources then that it has now.' Metisse picked up the narrative. 'This was more than two hundred years ago. The United States was in its infancy. It was a vast area with few people. The dark forests and mountains held no charm for the settlers. Only the Native American people lived here.'

'And the Wolves,' Charmaine added.

'Yes.' Metisse's voice was laced with venom. This happened every time they came up in a conversation. I wasn't sure why he was so adamant in his dislike of the Werewolves. Charmaine was much softer in her opinion.

'The Wolves were here when we came,' he continued. 'They mingled with the Native American tribes when they settled here long ago.'

Charmaine took his hand and softly stroked his fingers. He looked at her and smiled wryly. 'My mother and I do not share the same viewpoint regarding the Wolves.'

'Metisse still has the fire of territorial protection in his blood. He will eventually learn that fighting is not always the solution to everything.' She laughed.

'With the Wolves—it should be,' he answered vexed. To her repeated laughter.

I stayed mute. The animosity Metisse exhibited did not bode well for my plan. Or for my love life for that matter. I wondered where the hatred came from.

'The Wolves have just as much claim to this land as we do—more even—they were here first,' Charmaine lectured him. 'They do not have to be your enemy. They could even be your allies.'

I had to stop my mouth from dropping open. Was it possible Charmaine knew my plan? How could she? I'd told no one. Not yet. She didn't look at me or acknowledge my surprise. It must have shown in my eyes or the sharp intake of breath that followed her comment. Metisse hadn't noticed. He just made a wordless sound that showed his opinion on playing with his enemies.

'Times are changing, my son.' She looked up at him again. 'New times require re-evaluation of age-old beliefs. You will never be the clan leader you aspire to be if you hold on to your opinions with such stubbornness.' He stayed silent.

'And now it's time for this old lady to go to bed,' Charmaine declared. Immediately one of the guards stepped up to help her manoeuvre the electric chair to the back of the cabin where her bedroom was. 'Good night both of you. Sleep well.'

We replied with the same wishes and watched her leave. The guards both followed her to the suite and closed the door leaving us alone in the vast living room.

'Would you like a refill?' Metisse indicated my empty wine glass.

I shook my head. I reached my limit about two glasses ago.

His smile warmed me. I felt the familiar heat develop in my core. His boyish good looks and the mischievous sparkle in his eyes got me every time.

'How about we go to bed too?' he voiced my own thoughts.

I stood up from the sofa and had to steady myself as the wine took its toll. That elicited a laugh from my lover who hurried to catch me, exaggerating my inhibition to the max. I slapped his hands away and stood up more or less straight. I took a step towards the staircase, and he fell in behind me.

As I ascended the stairs, he pretended to support me, his hands on my butt. I'm sure that the kneading actions didn't really help me keep my balance as we giggled and laughed our way up to our bedroom. There we dropped onto the massive bed and proceeded to undress each other and ourselves.

The next morning, we lay in the glow of the sun as it filled the room with light through the floor-to-ceiling windows. It was glorious. I was tempted to just forget what I was here for.

Charmaine's company was a welcome addition to our little party, but her presence was also a distraction from what I needed to do. Metisse had to come to a meeting with the Wolves. With Gabriel to be exact. If last night's discussion was any indication, convincing him would be quite a chore. I felt him stir and turned over to look at him. He reluctantly let me change position. Metisse loved to spoon me. I enjoyed the feeling of protection it gave me, and it was usually the position we fell asleep in.

'Sleep well?' OK, it was corny, but I had to start somewhere. His face lit up with mischief.

'The few hours I managed to keep your hands off me, yes.'

I slapped his chest in mock anger and we both laughed. Our libidos were well suited to each other and even necessitated time apart to recuperate.

'It's beautiful here.' My comment was heartfelt. The view from the bed was magnificent. The deep autumn colours of the trees shone in the sunlight. I saw an eagle on the wing in the distance and wondered if it might be Ash—borrowing again.

Metisse just kissed the top of my head.

Man, I needed to get this done. Gathering all my courage I went for it. 'Do you trust me, Metisse?'

His brow creased, humour in his eyes. 'Now that's a stupid question. Of course I do. You are my soulmate. I trust you with my life.'

You might end up doing just that, I thought to myself. He looked a bit puzzled. Understandable. 'What brought that on?'

'There are things about me that you don't know,' I continued.

'Yes, and I'm looking forward to discovering them.' He smiled again.

Be careful what you wish for, I thought. These surprises might be quite different from what you expect.

'Some might not be what you imagine,' I tried to prepare him.

'OK.' Quizzical again. 'You going to explain what you're talking about? Because I have no idea.'

'Getting there,' I answered. 'It's not easy.' Right. Deep breath and jump in, I told myself.

'I'm not exactly who you think I am.' More creasing of the brow. 'I have a reason why I'm here in Waisland.'

'Yes, me.'

He was so narcissistic—in a sweet and endearing way. I recognised he was trying to lighten the mood.

'Besides you.' That was the right answer judging by his

smile of contentment. 'Seriously Metisse. I'm here because of a prophecy.' That got his attention.

'What prophecy?' He was all ears now. He turned fully towards me, supporting himself on his right elbow.

'One I can't exactly tell you everything about. But it has to do with the Council.'

He raised his left eyebrow at the comment about the Council. I hit a nerve. His eyes darkened and his face became rigid. All humour gone.

'What about the Council?' His voice had that familiar dark tone that surfaced when he was angry. I fully understood this anger. It was directed at the people who exiled his people and crippled his mother. He was fiercely protective of her and that made me wonder whether he had been at the battle where she was wounded.

I took another big breath and explained; 'the Council has oppressed the paranormal world long enough. It's time that we did something about it.'

He nodded his agreement. 'All of us,' I added. Still he nodded.

'There are many Sabre clans that would pick up arms,' he volunteered. 'We were not the only ones to be driven out of Canada or persecuted. Together we will be a formidable force.' I loved his enthusiasm and the way he immediately joined my cause. But once again, his scope was restricted to only the Sabres.

'All of us,' I repeated.

'Yes, I heard.'

'All of the paranormal creatures.'

That shut him up. I could almost feel the effort it took him to broaden his view to other creatures than his own kind. Metisse had a very elitist opinion of his clan and Sabres in general.

'What exactly do you mean with all of the paranormal creatures? Do you have a specific one in mind?' He chose his words carefully.

I nodded. Well, here goes nothing; 'yes, the Wolves.'

He threw up his hand and turned to lie on his back staring at the ceiling. Metisse took deep breaths in an attempt to calm himself. His body was almost in fight mode as his muscles tensed, just at the thought of the Wolves. This was not going to be easy.

I placed my hand on his chest and felt the strong beat of his heart. 'I know this is difficult for you,' I started.

'You have no idea,' he interrupted me.

'OK, so enlighten me. Why do you hate the Wolves so much?'

He was surprised. This was not the question he expected. But the air had to be cleared before I could go any further.

'You wouldn't understand,' he finally declared.

'Try me.' I wasn't letting him off that easily. He opened that can of worms, now he had to follow through.

He sighed in a way only a man can. I almost laughed, but he was deadly serious. I pulled myself together and put on a straight face. It was hard though.

'I was a teenager,' he started. 'This is one story my mother didn't tell you yesterday, because she doesn't know about it.' I doubted that but nodded to encourage him.

'Anyway. Some guys and I were in the forest hunting. We decided we would bag ourselves a deer. It was the first one we hunted alone—without the adults—so it had a lot of significance for us. We also made it into a kind of right-of-passage. We split up into twosomes and the first ones to bag a deer would win.'

He was already validating whatever was to come. I nodded again.

'We were stalking a doe, my friend Lucien and me. We got very close and were about to pounce when a pack of Wolves chased the doe away. There were about ten of them. I was mad as hell. We'd been watching the deer for more than an hour when the Wolves attacked, and all our work was for nothing. The pack was chasing it, so we had no chance of a kill anymore. Lucien tried to pull me back and whispered we should leave, but I refused. I stood up and shouted at the last Wolves. Two of them stopped and turned around. They paced back to us. Lucien ran off—the coward. I stayed put. I was the son of the clan leader and I wouldn't let any stupid mutt stare me down. It was our deer. Not theirs.'

He looked to me for validation. I was astounded. Surely this could not be the basis of his hatred? There must be more.

'Were the Wolves on clan territory?' I asked.

'That's beside the point.'

Ah, that would be a "no" then.

'We had our eye on the doe.' He was adamant in his righteousness.

'So did they.'

'You're taking their side?' The surprise and hurt was etched on his face.

'No, just stating the obvious,' I answered. 'Looks like you were both stalking the same prey.'

I was astounded he had not seen the Wolves. If they were there for an hour, then surely, they should have seen them stalk the deer too.

'Well, it was ours. And to make things worse, they beat me up.' Now he was really pouting like a small child.

I let it all sink in. 'And that is why you hate the Wolves so much?' I asked incredulously.

'Yes,' he said with less conviction than before.

'Do you know which wolf it was?'

'No. They were just at the back of the pack.' The omegas. An even bigger insult to a teenage ego.

'And this episode from your childhood, where you were on Wolf territory, hunting what was technically theirs, still clouds your judgement about the pack?' It wasn't really a question, and I could see Metisse understood.

He blushed heavily and averted his eyes. The small boy was still in there.

I wasn't holding my punches. This was the most ridiculous reason for years of animosity I had ever heard. And dangerous too. The wounded ego of a teenage boy would bring the two parties to the brink of war if Metisse actually had anything to say about the clan. These were the moments I was glad Charmaine was still the de-facto leader.

'You mean to say that all these years the strained relationship between you and the pack is the result of your wounded adolescent ego?' That landed. He blushed even deeper.

I took his face in my hands and kissed him softly on the lips. 'Metisse,' I said softly, 'I love you to bits. But grow up, will you?'

He half-smiled.

'Come on, how silly does that all sound?'

He tried to object, but finally had to concede that it was quite petty.

I became serious again. 'We need the Wolves, Metisse.'

'Why?'

'The Council will come down on us hard. We need

every hand, tooth and claw we can find. Besides it's better to have an ally than another enemy in the fight that's coming.'

'Yeah, but the Wolves?'

'Yes, the Wolves.'

My mind went back to last night's conversation in the living room. 'Your mother doesn't seem so averse to them as you are.'

'No, she never had problems with them.'

'Take an example from her, my love. And please open yourself up to cooperation. You don't have to become best friends. Just allies.' For now, I added silently. Somewhere deep inside I hoped that one day he and Gabriel might come to an understanding and, who knows, even start to vaguely like each other. I wasn't holding my breath. But I can dream, can't I?

'Will you come to a meeting with one of the Wolves?' I asked. 'At the clearing where your ancestors agreed to the treaty?'

'I'll have to think about it,' he answered dragging a decision. 'When is it?'

'Tomorrow at six pm.'

That didn't give him much time.

'Please, Metisse, do this for me.'

'Who will be there from the Wolves?' Curiosity got the better of him.

'Gabriel,' I answered.

'How did you get him to come?'

My turn to circumvent the questions. 'Please Metisse, just trust me, will you? All will become clear tomorrow.' I looked him straight in the eye. Willing him to comply. This was the basis of my plan. We had to get the Sabres and the Wolves to work together. That meant both of the leaders had to agree.

Another deep sigh.

'All right,' he finally said. 'But then you will tell me what is really going on here?' I nodded. 'And this is not an elaborate plan to get rid of me?'

I kissed him again. So that was the root of it all. He was scared he would lose me. 'Don't be silly,' I replied much to his relief. 'You're my soul mate.'

We kissed deeply, my lips and body convincing him in ways my words could not.

As an after-thought I added; 'oh, one more thing Metisse. Come alone. will you? Gabriel will as well.'

He nodded and turned his attention once more to my breasts.

One down. Now all I had to do was convince Gabriel.

Chapter Forty-Five

'Do you trust me, Gabriel?' I know, it wasn't original, but I was sticking to what worked with Metisse.

He looked at me. There was a sparkle in his eyes. The amusement spread to his lips and he smiled warmly, causing waves of tingles to run up and down my back as I lay in his arms in the after bliss of our lovemaking.

'Of course I do. You are my soulmate. I trust you with my life.'

That again. What was it with these guys that it always had to be a life-or-death thing? Couldn't they just say "yes." The way they said it only increased my sense of guilt. I was playing them. I knew it and felt bad—most of the time.

I admit, I loved the variation that these two gave me. They were very different lovers, and both fulfilled me. Now all I had to do was get rid of that nagging voice at the back of my mind that kept telling me that I was a bitch, and I was leading them both on.

'But you don't actually know me all that well,' I said carefully.

He took my hands, leaned over to me and kissed me lovingly. 'I know you well enough, my love. You would never intentionally hurt me. You are my life. My mate. I will be with you until the end of time.' The love spoke from his eyes, from the tender touch of his hands, and from the heat of his body against mine.

My heart skipped a beat. The devotion I saw in this man was astounding. He had waited for me all his very long life, and I was basically betraying him. He was my soulmate. I knew that. But so was Metisse. I didn't want to lose either of them. To be frank I loved them both. But would they agree with the situation I was going to propose? It would be a stretch. I had to believe that it was possible. Oh sure, I would survive any heartbreak. But they would not.

'There are things about me you don't know,' I tried to explain. I felt I owed him that. He had to know. He would soon anyway. I wanted to soften the blow. Because that was what it would be. A hell of a blow. I just hoped he would find it in his big heart to forgive me. Tears pushed at the back of my eyes.

'I know,' he surprised me. 'I know that I am not the only man with a claim to you.'

What? He knew, how could he?

'The moment that Ash took an interest in you, I knew that there was something special about you.' I let out my breath. He hadn't meant Metisse. \

'Ash said something about having waited for you. He knew you would come. That means there is a spiritual reason that you are here. I will have to share your time and attention with Ash.'

I felt so safe and content in his arms. So much so I entertained the thought of just dumping the whole plan and living my life here in the pack as Gabriel's mate. No more assassinations. No more prophecies. Just him and me.

That lasted for just about thirty seconds. Then reality reared its ugly head. The Council would never let Gabriel and Metisse live. They wanted them dead. If I didn't deliver on my assignment, I would join the guys on the death list. Peace and quiet was out of the question. And then there was my own private war with the Council. I would have my revenge.

'Penny for your thoughts,' Gabriel broke my dark thoughts.

I looked up at his face, the features I had come to love so much. He was such a kind- and warm-hearted man, no matter what image the town painted of him. No matter what the Sabres thought. I knew better.

I just smiled and kissed him. 'I love you.' There I'd finally said it out loud.

The effect was beautiful. His hand stroked the side of my face as he tried to say something. The emotions were just too much. There were tear drops in the corners of his beautiful grey eyes.

'You have no idea how much I needed to hear that.' His voice was soft, a whisper nearly. The tremor touched my heart. We kissed. Deep, full of promise. One thing led to another and we made beautiful passionate love. We took our time and focussed all our attention on the other.

'What's up?' Gabriel asked in the early afternoon. He had fallen into a deep peaceful sleep after our lovemaking while I stayed awake staring at the ceiling of the small cabin.

What possessed me to declare my love for him? Was it real, or just manipulative because I knew I had to convince him to do something against his nature? I searched deep inside my own mind and soul. Maybe it was just hopeful, but I decided my love was genuine. As was my declaration. Just those three words had a massive impact on Gabriel. They were a confirmation of the bond. It brought him peace of mind he hadn't thought possible anymore.

His hands softly stroked my hair as I snuggled up closer to him. I hadn't wanted to wake him, but I was glad that he was. I'd put this off for long enough. It was time to go to the next level in my plans.

'I need you to do something for me, Gabriel,' I said. 'And you're not going to like it.'

He cocked his head to the side and scrunched his brow. 'To make things worse,' I continued 'I can't tell you anything.'

'This is the thing you and Ash are working on?'

'Yes.' I could feel the smile. His hand continued to stroke my hair as he held me in his bear hug. 'I know that you have been to see him more than that one time I was there. You two are up to something. And that's what this is about?'

'It is. But…'

'I know. You cannot tell me everything about it.' Hmm, he had effectively circumvented the "anything" to "everything."

'How about a small peek?' he asked. I knew the curiosity was killing him. I stayed silent, debating what I could tell him. He deserved an explanation, just not all of it. Not just yet.

'I've guessed it has something to do with the Council,' he added giving me a handle on the issue.

'Yes,' I answered. 'It does.'

'OK, well that's good. It's about time someone did something about them. But what are we going to do?'

I loved the way he made it our problem, not just mine. He would do anything for me. I knew that. I felt it in his touch, saw it in the adoration in his eyes.

'First we need to gather a group of like-minded people.' I measured every word. Watching for an effect.

'That shouldn't be too hard. The Council has a lot of enemies.'

'Yes, but they would need to be willing to fight.'

'True. I think that shouldn't be too much of an issue,' he continued. 'People are fed up with the persecution and the way the council treats anyone who is not of their perceived status.'

'We will need allies,' I said again.

'Yes. I have contacts in the other packs. We should travel to them and propose your plan. Maybe bring Ash along as well. He has a lot of standing within the packs.'

His mind was going at a hundred miles, formulating plans to add more Werewolves to the forces. That was only part of what I wanted. The easy part.

'We might need to look further than just the packs,' I offered carefully.

He stayed silent for a few moments, then turned his body so that he looked into my face. There was concern there. And curiosity.

'Anyone specific?' Did I detect a slight edge to his voice there?

I took a deep breath and put it out there. 'The Sabres.'

'And that's the part I wouldn't like?' He continued to search my eyes. I hoped to God he didn't see all there was, not just yet. 'Why the Sabres?' he finally asked.

'Because they have numbers, power and money. And

they have a vested interest here in this territory. We don't need another enemy at the same time as the Council.'

He nodded. Yes, it made sense. But would that be enough to set aside the age-old differences? Not to mention the competition for me that he didn't know about yet.

Gabriel lay back down on the bed and pulled me close. I concentrated on his steady heartbeat and tried to calm my own nerves.

'I still think we should try the other packs first.'

'We'll do both,' I answered, relieved he hadn't written it off outright.

'Does Ash know?'

'Yes.' Ash knows everything.

'Figures. If anyone can get them to work with us, it's him. They owe him. Big time.'

Now the surprise was mine. Why did the Sabres owe Ash a debt? The big man wasn't telling me everything. Not that it was a surprise, he still adhered to the idea that I had to find it all out for myself. He was reluctant to offer unrequested information, preferring to answer my explicit questions. This was an interesting snippet of information he'd forgotten to mention. I will have to ask him about that.

'Would you please come to a meeting with me? Just you, me, Ash and Metisse.' I held my breath.

He looked me deep in the eyes, searching for answers to obvious questions, like how did I know Metisse? I held his stare, trying to portray the importance of the meeting in my eyes. Gabriel was tuned to body language, maybe even more than to spoken word.

He nodded. 'When?'

'In about two hours.' I was cutting it close. We had to meet today and get this all organised before Alex came back from the Council. No way could I have him sticking his nose into my business until I'd convinced my lovers to work together.

Gabriel smiled. 'Wow, no pressure then. Where?'

'In the clearing where the first treaty was created.'

'Good choice.' He's much more perceptive than Metisse. That's understandable, he has seen more and is infinitely wiser.

'That means we have about another hour before we have to leave.' His eyes sparkled again. I nodded and pulled him closer. We would get through the wait one way or the other.

Chapter Forty-Six

As I planned, we got there before Metisse. Ash turned up about ten minutes later in a worn-out pick-up truck that looked as though it should have been scrapped decades ago. The deep rumble of the engine belied the exterior. There was some real power underneath that hood.

Ash greeted Gabriel, then came over and kissed me on the cheek. He had to bend over to do so, and as always, I felt like a small child next to such a big man.

His mohawk was more muted in colour than the last time I saw him and decorated with two eagle feathers. A souvenir of his last borrowing maybe?

The clearing boasted an astounding view of the mountains and the forests. The woodland surrounding us was dark and deep, the trees close together. The afternoon sun lit up the clearing and warmed us as we waited for Metisse. It was totally private, secluded and off the beaten path. There would be no casual passers-by. This was exactly what we needed.

I felt the history of this place, the hairs on the back of

my neck tingled with every breeze. I imagined the souls of those who negotiated the first treaty between the Sabres and the Wolves were here with us. Looking at both Gabriel and Ash I had the profound feeling they felt the presences too. Ash must have. He was attuned to this kind of things. And he might even have been there, for all I knew.

I couldn't stand still. Every thirty seconds I scanned the track that led to the clearing, searching for the headlights of Metisse's car. None came. Gabriel observed me with mirth and more than a bit of confusion. He walked up to me and took me into his arms. As much as I appreciated his warmth and empathy, me in this position might not be a good starting point for the discussions if Metisse suddenly turned into the clearing. I kissed him to thank him and we walked over to Ash. He stood on one side of the Shaman and I took up a spot on the left.

'It will be ok.' Ash's calm and deep voice was soothing. But there was no way any words he or Gabriel could say would calm my nerves. And justly.

I was only now becoming aware of the extent of my deceit. I had led both of these wonderful men on. Sure, they were both my soul mates, but they were completely unaware of the fact they shared me. Both were convinced they were the only one. This could get very ugly.

Finally, about twenty minutes late, we heard the rumble of a large SUV as it made its way up the path. The deep boom was smooth, unlike that of Ash's car. It had an almost fluid quality. The headlights lit up the dark track into almost daylight as the car turned into the open space. The sun threw long shadows as it started to disappear behind the high trees. There was more than enough light to see, but it would be twilight soon.

The car stopped twenty metres from where we stood. I

waited as the engine shut off and the door opened. My breath escaped in a sigh when I recognised Metisse as he stepped out from behind the door of the SUV. Somehow, I hadn't really expected him to come.

He looked at us standing there. His gaze travelled from Ash to Gabriel. The yellow glow in his eyes belied his calm exterior. When he saw me, he smiled warmly. I felt both happy and completely embarrassed at the same time.

My guilt showed. I tried to smile, but his quizzical gaze showed I hadn't been convincing.

Ash's hand touched my elbow, encouraging me to continue what I had started. I was grateful for his support. My first instinct was to turn and run. His touch reminded me of why we were all here.

I glanced over at Gabriel. The fire in his eyes was a clear indication that he knew part of what was going on here. He'd pieced together that Metisse and I were more than acquaintances. The loving way Metisse acknowledged me wasn't lost on Gabriel.

Metisse remained where he was. The puzzlement was clear on his face. He had no idea what was going on here. He must have felt the tension. Maybe he possessed an inbuilt mechanism to stop him from coming to unwanted conclusions, it would explain a lot. I walked over to him and took his hands.

'Thank you for coming, Metisse.'

'Sure,' he answered uncertainly.

When I didn't expand on the situation, he cocked his head in question. Being the coward that I am, I just turned and, hand in hand, led him to the other two.

If looks could kill, I think none of us would still be alive. Not even me. Though I might just be collateral damage.

I let go of Metisse's hand and took up a place between

both of my lovers. We made up a triangle of sorts. All about one-and-a-half to two metres from each other. Ash took a step backwards to give us space. Metisse and Gabriel observed each other, then stole glances at me.

'What the hell is going on here, Trish?' Gabriel finally asked. Metisse nodded almost imperceptibly.

Metisse and Gabriel stood opposite each other. Their negative energy heated the air. Sparks actually pushed the goose bumps up my arms in waves.

Here we were, my two beaus and me. All in one place. The two people I kept apart for weeks were now no more than two metres apart. The only thing that stopped them from ripping each other apart was their love for me. I brought them here. Convinced both of them to listen to what I had to say. To stay all aggression until they knew what my plans were.

I didn't need to tell them they were both my lovers. They deduced that from the vibes in the air and the looks both shot at me. What I said would just be a validation.

That was the first surprise, and not a welcome one for either of them. Yeah, well, get used to it. This was how it was, and how it was going to be. I ran by my own rules. And if that meant that I had two men, then that was my prerogative.

I think it was hardest on Gabriel. He was the alpha of a more male dominated society. This idea of a woman running the show was alien to him. Metisse clearly under-stood the strength of women. He had a perfect example—Charmaine, his mother. But still, he wasn't acting like it.

In the background I saw the clan and pack members between the trees. I had asked both men to come alone. Well, so much for my influence.

The only other person in the clearing was Ash. He was

as calm as ever. I couldn't read him, and despite the fact I trusted him beyond my life, it still made me apprehensive.

'This place is starting to smell of wet dog.' Trust Metisse to fling the first insult. The amused and condescending smile on his face was in stark contrast to the raw hatred Gabriel projected.

The atmosphere in the clearing was volatile. I tasted the tension. One way or the other I needed to defuse the situation before it got out of hand. I admit I'd underestimated the effect the two rivals would have on each other. That and the fact they knew they both had a claim to me.

Another thing I didn't take into account was the childish behaviour both of them—but mostly Metisse—displayed.

Chapter Forty-Seven

I was about to rebuke them when my attention was distracted by the deep growl of a heavy V8 engine.

The familiar deep black custom Dodge Van pulled up to the clearing. The driver stepped out and opened the rear doors. With a wiring sound a ramp descended from the back of the vehicle and connected to the ground.

I waited with bated breath. What was this? Why would Charmaine be here? I looked at Ash. He observed the van with a big smile on his face. He obviously knew more about what was happening than I did. I would have to speak to him about this later. This was my show—remember?

Another humming sound came from the van and the electric wheelchair made its way down the ramp. Charmaine expertly turned the chair, raised the seat upwards so her face was at the same level as ours and made her way over the clearing towards where we stood.

'Mother?'

Right, so it wasn't Metisse who had organised this. The

surprise on his face was genuine. His brow was crunched in bewilderment, his mouth open, not knowing what to say or how to react. He looked at me. I shrugged. I had no idea myself.

Ash walked over to Charmaine and took her proffered hand. He brought her hand to his lips and kissed her fingers lightly.

'Charmaine, so good of you to come.' Well, that answered that question. She was here on the Shaman's request.

'Of course, Ash. It is finally time.'

Now what the hell did that mean? And why did I get the impression the real power in this area of the world was now complete. Plus, Ash and Charmaine obviously knew each other. Not only that, but they were also on speaking—and hand kissing—terms.

There were smiles all around. At least between those two. I was lost. I had no idea what was going on.

Charmaine turned to the two men in my life. 'Son,' she acknowledged Metisse. 'You might want to close your mouth,' she joked. The surprise was still etched on his face. He could only nod as he did as he was told.

'Gabriel,' she said with more warmth in her voice that I expected. This was her arch-rival. Her would-be nemesis if it came to a war. Or was he? Everything I thought I knew just become questionable.

'My lady,' he answered with a small bow.

OK. Now I really had no clue what was happening. But I would have to run with it whatever.

'Trish, my dear.' She turned to me.

'Hallo, Charmaine.' I couldn't help myself. 'I didn't expect to see you here.'

'No,' she answered with a small chuckle. 'I expect you didn't. Ash invited me to this monumental event.'

I cocked my head in question, but she didn't explain further. She just smiled. Right. No explanations there either. I decided to get back to what I, and all the others were here for.

It was my mantra; "when flustered: bluff."

I turned my attention back to my two lovers.

I looked into Gabriel's eyes. The pupils had changed from his usual grey to jet black with red rims and were fully dilated. A sure sign he was mad as hell. Well, tough. Shit happens.

Glancing at Metisse, I saw he wasn't doing much better. It's not just the fact they were both vying for my love, these two were life-long, natural enemies.

It's the cat and dog thing.

There couldn't be more of a difference between two people than here. They embodied the extremes with regard to lifestyle, status, outlook in life. One had it all, the other fought for every dime. What they did have in common was their unwavering loyalty towards their families.

Metisse had the clan. Gabriel had his pack. Both would do anything to guarantee the safety of their kin.

And then there was me. They had me in common. Only that wasn't their choice. It was mine.

I'd grossly misjudged the impact the close proximity would have. They looked ready to attack each other.

Both stole glances at Ash and Charmaine. Like me, they were stumped by the ease in which the two unwritten leaders of the groups communicated. They seemed comfortable with each other. Almost good friends. How the hell did that happen? Nothing ever hinted at what I was seeing now. Gabriel seemed slightly less surprised. He knew more. I would have to talk to him after we sorted this out. If we were still on speaking terms, that is.

Metisse was so sure of himself. His arrogance was part of what attracted me to him. But here he was playing a dangerous game. Sure, if push came to shove and Metisse and Gabriel went at it, Metisse would probably win. Once shifted, he was bigger and much more dangerous in a one-on-one fight. But one-on-one wasn't the pack's way. They had strength in numbers. The damage they could do to Metisse as a group would be extensive. If their adversary were alone that is, and he wasn't either. I could see the bright yellow eyes between the trees. Three, probably more of Metisse's clan had come to protect their boss. More likely they'd come spoiling for a fight, just for the fun of it. There were Werewolves on the right and Sabretooths on the left. It would be a hell of a fight. If it ever came down to that.

I wasn't against a rumble to relief the stress. I just didn't think their oversized male egos and testosterone overloads would let them stop before they killed each other. And frankly, that would defeat my purpose. Like I said, I'm greedy. I want them both. Preferably with all their limbs attached. Plus, I have a plan. One, I need both of them alive for.

That made it time to intervene.

'Guys.' I walked down to stand between the two like a referee in a boxing match—a boxing match with an abundance of claws and fangs.

Metisse smiled at me as I passed him, his hand softly brushed my arm. His bright yellow eyes lit up with pleasure at seeing me. The white of his beautiful teeth showed between his lips, the slight points of the descending Sabre canines the only indication he was not exactly at ease here.

Gabriel was much more open in his feelings. I could

read them off his face in the dark scowl that stayed put as I looked him in the red-rimmed eyes. These was no relaxation there. His body inclined slightly my way—finally a reaction to my presence—but he fought the pull and retained his defiant stance leering over his six-centimetre shorter adversary. My hand on his arm didn't help soothe the anger, I felt the tense muscles beneath the denim shirt.

The tension was palpable in the air around the three of us. Even I started to doubt whether this was a good idea. But I'd made my choice and now it was time to persevere. My "master plan" was about to come to its full potential. I glanced at Ash and Charmaine for a bit of support. Ash nodded almost imperceptibly while Charmaine smiled. Well, here goes nothing.

'Cut the macho crap, will you.' I usually appreciated the manly stuff, but now it was getting on my nerves. Besides, it was counterproductive. These two had to stop imagining ways of killing each other. Co-existence was the key now.

They both screwed up their faces, the eyebrows lifting in surprise and disbelief. Especially Gabriel. He was not used to being talked back to. Not that it made any difference to me. I knew what I wanted and theirs was a "yes" or "no" answer.

'Back off.' I physically pushed them further apart. My strength was the first surprise. In all my dealing with each of them I'd never let them experience my actual physical strength. I always held back, sometimes even played the weak female if expected. Now, there was no reason to keep up the premise. Not from my perspective. It was all or nothing.

The tone of my voice must have registered. Even through the macho posturing Gabriel portrayed so convincingly. Slowly he took a step back, making sure I understood that it was his idea. Whatever. It made no difference to me. If that was what it took; great.

Metisse stayed put until I locked eyes with him. He backed off. Reluctantly—but he did. Good idea. My patience was at an all-time low.

Chapter Forty-Eight

I took a deep breath, gathered my frayed nerves, looked at them both, then stole another glance at Ash and went for it. 'You have a right to be mad,' I started. 'I owe you both an explanation.' Gabriel nodded, Metisse just glared. 'In fact, all of you,' I added, including Charmaine in the discussion. She just smiled, strengthening my hunch she knew much more about what was happening. Maybe even more than I did.

'I came to Waisland on a mission.' Man, this was hard. I underrated the influence their and my emotions would have on me, and now I was paying the price. It all seemed so logical and practical this morning. I would just explain, and they would agree. Ideally shake hands and both continue to love me. God, I was naive.

'The Council sent me.'

'What?' Metisse was flabbergasted. He turned his full attention to me. 'You're here on the Council's orders?'

Gabriel was quieter, more dangerous. 'What for?' he asked.

'To kill you both,' I answered bluntly. The reaction was as expected. They both looked puzzled, Gabriel took a step back, then realised what he had done when he saw the pain on my face and came back to his original position.

'You're here to kill us?' his voice was almost a whisper. 'Is that why we're here? Now?'

'No, No. I could never kill you,' I said to him, heartbroken. I turned to Metisse. 'Or you.'

I felt tears at the edge of my eyes. If I could have just faded away from Metisse's glare and Gabriel's intense scowl, I would have. My body shrank a bit, my back no longer straight and proud. I clutched my hands in each other, trying to get hold of myself. I had to. I came this far. To leave it like this would mean I'd lost everything. Everyone.

I stood up straight, sniffed back the tears and looked them both in the eyes. There, behind the anger, I could still see the love they had for me. That was what I had to keep in mind.

'That was my mission,' I continued, my voice getting stronger with each word. 'I was a Council Assassin.'

'Was?' Gabriel asked.

'Yes. Was. The only reason I did what I did was to get close to the Council so that I could find out who there was responsible for my mother's death and finally exact my revenge. It was a means to an end. You both were my last mission.'

'Why?' Gabriel was the only one to actually ask questions. Metisse looked dumbstruck.

'The oracle Aquanaris had a vision. You both would start a war between the Sabres and Werewolves that would expose the paranormal world to the humans. It had to be prevented. The usual Council solution is to kill off the leaders of both of the factions that threaten the war. They didn't know who would be responsible, just that it would happen soon. I was sent to find out who and stop them before the war started.' I let that sink in.

'How did you find us?' Metisse finally found his voice. 'And why would we start a war?'

'You wouldn't,' I answered to his surprise. 'The longer I've been here, the more I realised there were other reasons why the Council wanted you dead. It wasn't because of a war between you two. It was a war between the Council and the oppressed paranormal world. The oracle foresaw the demise of the Council, and I was sent to prevent it from happening.'

It was a lot to take in. I realised that. Gabriel became silent, I desperately wanted to know what was going on in his mind. He shielded any body language, and I was shut out. It felt like a stab to the heart.

'I started off this mission as just that, a job. Then I met you both. I didn't count on getting emotionally involved. It happened. Twice.'

Metisse just stared at me. The conflict in his face was apparent in the rapid blinking of his eyes. Gabriel refused to look at me.

'I know it's hard to take…'

'You have no idea,' Gabriel whispered. His words cut me to the bone. 'After hundreds of years I thought I'd finally found my soul mate. Someone who would love me as I did her. And now you say it was a hoax. That you played me? That none of it was real?'

'That's not what I said,' I almost shouted desperately.

I took a deep breath. I needed to pull myself together. Get a hold on what was happening. Get them to understand.

I continued in a more controlled voice. 'The feelings I

have for you and Metisse are legitimate and undeniable. Believe me I've tried to ignore them. To regale my emotions to stupid hormones. But they run much, much deeper. You are part of my soul Gabriel. And so is Metisse. I don't know why—I just know that you both are.'

He looked up, I saw the pain in his eyes and felt tears run down my cheeks. He was so completely hurt it distressed me intensely. I cringed at his anguish.

'Loving you was never a lie,' I said softly. 'You are my soulmate. There is no denying that. You feel it in your bones, and so do I.' I saw hope in his eyes.

'Where does that leave me?' Metisse angrily interrupted.

'In exactly the same place,' I answered.

'What the fuck does that mean?' His anger flared even higher. 'You said that you loved ME. That you were MY soulmate. And now this.' He spread his hands out to encompass me and Gabriel. 'Now you declare your commitment to him.' The last words were emphasised. 'You lied to me about your love.'

'No, Metisse. I didn't.' I reached out to touch his arm, but he shrugged me off violently. 'I never lied to you about my feelings for you. You are also my soulmate.'

'Fuck that.'

He was piping mad. His eyes burned bright yellow. The points of his Sabre teeth showed from under his top lip. 'How could you? I trusted you. My mother did.' That hurt. 'And you lied to us all.'

'Leave me out of it, Metisse, just listen to what Trish has to say.' Charmaine intervened. Her words were like a soft balm to me. Something I desperately needed.

'Yes, Metisse. I lied to you. About my work. About why I was in Waisland. I never lied to you about my love for you,' I answered his allegations.

His mouth contorted in a half growl. 'So, all the days you weren't with me. You were fucking this mongrel?'

He was doing his best to make me hurt as much as he did. I understood his attitude, but it still pained me. I also expected more from him. More maturity. He was acting like a child. So petty and egotistical.

I felt Gabriel tense beside me. I put my hand on his arm to calm him. Thankfully, he didn't pull away. This was going downhill fast. I had to get a hold on it. On Metisse, before he started the war I was supposedly sent to stop.

'Metisse.' My voice must have been full of the menace that I felt, because he shut his mouth before he could utter what he was about to say. 'Yesterday, when we talked, I told you to grow up. Now would be a good time to start.'

We stood like that for at least two minutes. It was a stand-off. I stayed silent. It was up to them to see if they could digest what I had just said.

'Why are we here?' Gabriel broke the silence. 'It's not just so you can explain this triangle thing.'

'No,' I replied. I was so grateful to Gabriel. I knew this was not the end of the discussion, but he had decided to park it until a later time. 'I realised that the Council was playing me. Using me to stop the revolution they knew was coming. I was confused. Then Gabriel took me to see Ash and things fell into place.'

Both men turned to look at Ash. He nodded his agreement. I wish I possessed his calm demeanour. Maybe just a little bit of it would rub off on me. I concentrated on his multicoloured eyes. It helped before. They soothed me. I felt the muscles in the back of my neck relax ever so slightly, then the knot at the base of my skull. Just a little…

'It sounds like a load of bull shit,' Metisse interrupted bluntly.

He turned his attention from me to Gabriel. Disdain was written across his face as he looked down his nose at the biker. His eyes travelled from the boots, over the black jeans, leather jacket up to the cold, red-rimmed eyes in Gabriel's hard face.

It looked like my comment about growing up hadn't registered in Metisse's thick skull. Gabriel didn't take the bait, he stood calmly, and I truly believe that irritated Metisse even more. I suspect that was why Gabriel was acting this way. The complete lack of respect screamed at his adversary in the contempt with which he viewed Metisse.

I was at a loss what to do at that moment. Testosterone ruled whatever was happening here now. Any common sense left the scene in a hurry.

Slowly I felt heat rising along my spine past my shoulders and up my neck tensing all the muscles again and sending a bolt of pain into my brain. Sure, I knew I wasn't handling this well, but I'd explained as much as they would let me. Now they were acting like stupid adolescents. Anger pushed away the guilt and pain. Anger at myself for approaching it all wrong and even for letting things get this far. But also anger at them. At their stupid egos. Their ridiculous feuds. These weren't cats and dogs. They were much more evolved than that. It was time they started to act like rational beings.

Something had to change. Quickly.

I lowered my voice to almost a whisper. The sound of my words registered even more menace than shouting would.

'Yes, I was wrong to get involved with both of you. At this moment, with you two acting the way you are, I'm starting to regret both of my relationships.'

They stared at me. 'You are surprised. Hurt. I get it. Believe it or not, this is painful to me too.'

Metisse was about to say something but stopped open mouthed when I lifted my hand between us and closed my eyes. 'As I said, I didn't plan this. None of it. It was supposed to be a quick mission, in and out. Two dead and me back to what was really important to me. The one thing that has dominated my life since I was twelve. Revenge for my mother's death. There hasn't been a day that I haven't felt the total isolation of loss ever since the Council took her. She died saving me. Revenge was all I had. All I needed. It was what I breathed day and night. It shaped my actions and my thoughts. It was what I lived for.'

I took a deep breath.

'Then I came here, and everything changed—everything. I thought I could live without love. I had for many decades. I pushed it to the back of my mind. Hardened my heart and lived on the memories of my mother's love for me. The one thing that had ultimately killed her.'

I paused. This was more information than I wanted to share, but now that the lid was off, I couldn't stop myself. 'And then I met you. Both of you. And what happened after that screwed up all my plans. Love is painful. It burns and tears at me. Loving you both is killing me. The guilt, the way it affects you, what I'm doing to you. I know. I feel it. And I can't do anything else than what I'm doing now.'

No one spoke. We stood in the clearing as the sun slowly set behind the trees and enhanced the eerie feelings I had. Even the sound of the nocturnal animals stilled. My whole body tingled. I felt the blood flow and my heart pound. I closed my eyes and willed my body to compose itself. Hoping against hope I wouldn't break down and cry. Pain and anger tore at me in equal amounts. It threatened to break my restraints. Slow breaths. In. Out. Rest. In. Out. Rest. And again.

Slowly my raging heart calmed, the stabbing pain behind my eyes receded and I felt the knots in my muscles unravel. With another deep breath I raised my head and looked first at Gabriel, then at Metisse.

Chapter Forty-Nine

'Again. What are we doing here?' Gabriel at least caught on to the fact there was a reason why they were at a stand-off. Good for him. He seemed to be more intelligent than I credited him for. 'Is this a coincidence?' Hmm, not so clever after all, 'or did you orchestrate this?' Orchestrate; now that sounded good. Like I really thought this through. I had— well part of it.

'No coincidences,' I answered. 'I got you both here for a reason.'

'And what would that be?' Metisse asked, his voice was laced with sarcasm. His eyes turned to me; the smile painted on his lips was wavering.

'Me,' I said quasi-enthusiastically. Blank faces again. Metisse's eyebrow lifted as he cocked his head to the side. Gabriel hunched his shoulders briefly. Did I really have to spell it all out? Seems like I did.

'As you've figured out by now, I have a relationship with both of you.' Snarls and killing looks at each other. Guys. Grow up!

'You both have a claim to me, as your mate.' That registered. Identical creased brows in question. 'And I to you.'

'How is that possible?' Metisse finally said. 'You cannot be mated to a mutt.'

Low growls in support of their alpha echoed from the right side of the forest. Answering rumbles resounded from the Sabres on the left.

'Stop the insults Metisse. You're above that kind of thing,' Charmaine intervened. My lover's chocolate skin blushed even darker as he averted his eyes.

I was astounded they hadn't figured it out by now. Was it that difficult to get their head around? Or were they just reluctant to see what was right under their eyes.

'Gabriel,' I asked. 'What am I according to you?' He looked at me incredulously. I nodded and smiled to encourage him to answer.

'You're half Wolf and half human,' he stated.

'Metisse.' I turned toward the Sabre. 'What do you think that I am?'

'Easy. You're half Sabre and half human,' Metisse was quick to answer.

'Well, you are both half right.'

They both turned their face towards me, surprise and incomprehension in their visages.

I continued, 'but there's a problem there. Isn't there? Half Wolf, half Sabre and half human. That's one half too many. And guess what I definitely am not?' I paused. 'Human.'

I let that sink in.

'What the hell do you mean?' Metisse exclaimed. 'How can you not be part human?' I wanted to help him, but kept my mouth shut. 'It's impossible. There's no other option.'

'Yes, there is.' Gabriel's deep voice came through clearly.

He'd figured it out. Again, it made me think he had more background information. The cogs in Metisse's brain creaked as he struggled to come to terms with the only explanation for the riddle. He knew, just didn't want to accept it.

'You can't be,' he finally said as realisation took hold. 'It's not possible.'

I nodded. So did Gabriel. Metisse shook his head, closed his eyes, then looked at me again. I kept my face as it was. He looked at his mother, at Ash. Things were finally falling into place.

'The prophecy,' Gabriel whispered. I placed my hand on his arm, so happy he had figured it all out.

'What prophecy?' Metisse's voice was raised, not in anger, more in frustration. He had no idea what was going on. Charmaine rolled up to her son, elevated the chair and placed her hand on his shoulder in support. It was a lot to take in.

'Don't tell me you never heard of the Lamaq?' Gabriel asked his adversary. The lines on Metisse's brow deepened as he tried to understand what Gabe implied. His eyes opened wider, his lips parted, and his tongue licked the top lip quickly in a nervous manner.

'It's a myth,' he finally answered. The tone was more of a question than a statement. He glanced at his mother who nodded at him.

'Is it?' I smiled.

'Of course, it is.' Metisse answered his own question.

'It isn't,' Gabriel said flatly. 'It's true. The living proof is standing here in front of you. Trish is the prophecy.'

Metisse shook his head and closed his eyes, his brow creased with the effort. 'No,' he stated resolutely. 'No, it's not possible.'

'It is,' Charmaine interceded. 'You must open your mind, my son. You know. Now you must accept.'

He opened his eyes and looked at her, silently begging her to say that it wasn't so. He knew about the Lamaq. The one of two worlds, who would bring the paranormals together and join them in a common cause.

'That's you?' He looked at me.

'Yes,' I answered softly. This was difficult. I understood that. It had taken me a long time to accept it. I glanced at Gabriel. He'd already resigned himself to my hybrid heritage.

'How is this possible?' Metisse asked me.

'My mother was Sabre, that you know. My father was a Werewolf,' I explained.

'How long have you known?' Gabriel asked?

'Known that I was a hybrid?' I asked in turn. 'I've known I was different all my life. My hybrid heritage? Since I was twelve. I grew up with just my mother. We were always running. Never stayed in one place for long. I never knew my father. He abandoned us when I was a baby. Couldn't handle the stress, I guess.'

'That's not exactly true,' Ash intervened.

Chapter Fifty

Now the surprise was on my side. We all turned towards Ash. He stepped forward and joined our little group. I didn't know what to say. I always believed my father abandoned us—left my mother and me to fend for ourselves and evade the Council's assassins. It was cut-and-dry as far as I was concerned. Typical male commitment angst. It was one of the main reasons why I never committed to any relationship. Up till now.

Now I had two. Go figure.

'Trish.' The tall man squeezed my shoulder in support. 'Your father never abandoned you and your mother. He couldn't—he loved you both more than life itself. That was why he left. Because of love.'

I just gaped at him. No words came out of my mouth.

Now that was a first. I couldn't remember ever being lost for words. The sting of tears threatened to push through my resolve. I would not cry. Never. Not in front of others. My pain was for solitary moments. I gathered my dignity and stared into his beautiful multi-coloured eyes, looking for the peace that I found there before.

'Then why?' I whispered. Why had he left? Why hadn't he helped us when we needed him so much? When I needed a father.

'Your parents were very much in love. Theirs was love that transcended all boundaries. Man-made and divine. They were ecstatic when you were born. You were the apotheosis of their love.'

He made it sound so wonderful. Then why was I alone now? Where were they?

'Others were not so enamoured,' he continued. 'Your father was a very important man in the Wolf community. He was ancient, almost as old as I am, with the knowledge and wisdom of his years. Ishmael quickly understood the dire straits his small family was in.'

'Ishmael?' Gabriel was astounded. 'Her father's Ishmael?'

Ash nodded.

'Who is Ishmael?' I demanded with more anger than I wanted. How come everyone here knew more about me than I did? I was getting seriously pissed off. This was not how I envisioned the meeting to go.

'Ishmael was one of the founding Wolves,' Ash explained.

'One of the first,' Gabriel added just in case I didn't understood the gravity of it all.

'The first?'

'Yes.' Ash squeezed my shoulder again. 'There were initially three. He was one of them.' I let that sink in. So, I was the descendant of Werewolf royalty, if there were such a thing. This was getting weirder every minute.

'You were saying?' I needed to know more about why he had left. 'About why?'

'Ishmael received word the Council was looking for a hybrid. The oracle had a vision.'

'Aquanaris?' Dread sent shivers up and down my spine. Her again.

'Yes, Aquanaris. She had foreseen that a hybrid of Sabre and Wolf would unite the clans and packs and bring down the Council. The child of the two worlds would bring an end to the tyranny and free the paranormal world. The Council sent their assassins to find such a child. Ishmael knew if he stayed with you and your mother it would be the same as painting a target on your backs. The Sabres and Wolves weren't traditionally allies. They warred for territories. Adversaries at best. Enemies at worst. A highly placed Wolf travelling with an equally esteemed Sabre and a small child would be too conspicuous. They had to split up. There was no way they could stay together and live. Your mother reluctantly agreed. It was the only way to keep you safe.'

'That was when they came to you?'

'It was. They wanted to know the truth behind the prophecy Aquanaris foretold.'

'And you validated it.' It wasn't a question. No answer was needed.

I tried to absorb what he'd said. And what it meant.

All my life I lived under the conviction my father hadn't loved me. That he deserted us. My mother never said so. It was a conclusion I made on my own. It was the only one that made sense to me for all those years. It was an explanation for something I desperately needed to understand. My mother never told me who my father was. Just that he was a Wolf, and their union was frowned on. That they could not stay together. Two days before I lost her, she told me about the prophecy and why we were being hunted.

I never really believed I was some kind of super being destined to bring about the release of the oppressed supernatural world. It sounded like a fairy tale—a bad one at that—and I banished it to the back of my mind. Now it was back with a vengeance.

Sure, Ash had convinced me the prophecy was what drove the Council. But still, I did not truly believe it. Now I was faced with the fact that my parents had both acted on the conviction I was indeed the chosen one. They accepted the prophecy as truth.

And now it was my turn.

'What happened to my father?' My question was barely audible.

'Two years after your parents split up, the Council came for Ishmael. We believe Aquanaris had a more detailed vision that identified your parents. They started to hunt them—you—with a vengeance after that. Ishmael managed to evade the Council for another year until a group of assassins cornered him. We have not heard from him since. We must presume he is no longer with us.'

Dead.

Just when I started to warm to the idea I had a real father, he was gone. This was quickly going downhill. My initial elation that he once loved me, crashed into an enormous pain with the knowledge he was dead. I was never able to get to know him, and now it was too late. I was basically an orphan. Both my parents were gone. Dead at the hands of the Council. How was I to continue after that? How could I cope with the pain?

Where to start?

Help came from an unexpected source. Charmaine wheeled her chair towards me, she took my trembling hands in hers.

'Your parents truly loved you, my dear.' Her words were both soothing and killing. My parents loved me so much that they were both dead. Because of me. The tears started to leak from the side of my eyes down over my cheeks, despite my resolve.

'You are not the reason they are no longer here,' she continued as she wiped away the tears on the side of my face. 'They knew the dangers. They knew they had to keep you safe, not only for them, but for all of us.'

'How do you know?' I whispered.

'She was my dear friend.' Another bombshell. 'We grew up together in Canada. Not from the same clan, but neighbours. She and I stayed in contact after the Council scattered the Canadian Sabres. I saw her last when she came here with Ishmael and you.'

There was so much I didn't know. Things I had to find out.

'I've lost both of them,' I finally said after digesting the news.

I looked at Charmaine, the warmth in her face made me feel slightly less alone. Both Gabriel and Metisse fought the urge to take me in their arms. It would have been difficult to decide which one I would have gone to. I turned to Ash, he looked as though he wanted to say something. I cocked my head in question. He shook his head, with a small smile on his lips.

OK, I would have to get back to him about that later. Find out what it was Ash wasn't telling me.

Right. It was time to pull myself together and get down

to business. This was not what I was here for. I would have time later to catch up with everyone who knew my parents. There would be tears. And maybe there would be closure.

Now, we had to get down to business.

Chapter Fifty-One

I straightened my back, took a deep breath and prepared myself to take back control of this meeting.

'Thank you all for your support.'

My voice still sounded a bit off; wobbly. I coughed to clear my throat, swallowed and started again.

'I appreciate it.' That was better. I sounded more in control. 'I have questions, but they will have to wait. It's not what we are here for now.'

Ash and Charmaine glanced at each other and smiled. I was back. She manoeuvred back towards Ash.

I turned to my two beaus. It was time to lay down the new law here. Neither of them was stupid. They should have connected the dots by now.

'Where was I? Right. I'm half Sabre and half Wolf. That makes me unique. It also makes you acknowledge me as your mate. Both of you.' I looked at them both pointedly.

'How can you be mate to us both?' Gabriel asked confused. 'It's unheard of.'

'Not exactly,' Ash intervened again. 'It happens—not often—but there are cases where a mate has been shared.'

'Between species?' Metisse added his two cents sarcastically.

'No, not between species,' Ash had to add honestly. 'But then again. There have never been times like these.'

'It's not possible,' Gabriel claimed. 'We are enemies. We cannot even share the same territory; how do you expect us to share a mate?' The anger resurfaced. The red glint was back in his now dark eyes.

Looking at him, I loved the way he fought for me. Metisse too. He nodded his agreement. See, they could agree on something. Just not the right thing.

'You are opponents,' Ash corrected. 'And even that can change. You do not need to be enemies. Ishmael and Embre proved that. Now would be a prudent time to set aside your differences and join forces. We all have a mutual enemy; the Council. We will need to work together to take them on.'

Metisse scoffed at the remarks. 'We do not need the mutts help for anything.' The arrogance was back full fling. Charmaine scowled at his bad manners. Gabriel, miraculously, refrained from reacting. He was watching me.

'Besides,' Metisse continued, gaining in confidence, 'you're more Sabre than anything else.' He couldn't bring himself to say half Wolf. 'You even shift, fully.'

'I shift into a Sabre or a Wolf.' I burst his bubble. 'And both.' To prove my point, I shifted my left arm into a tawny Sabre paw, and my right into the deep black I became as a Wolf.

Metisse was clearly flustered. He couldn't believe his eyes. I think he didn't want to acknowledge what he could no longer ignore.

Gabriel just stood there. His face calm and composed.

He didn't react to the change or to Metisse's nervous fidgeting. He just waited.

I took strength from him. The reactions were completely opposite to what I expected. Metisse's world was more contemporary. Gabriel's was steeped in tradition, with fixed roles for all pack members. I had expected him to hold onto what he knew, the structure and very fibre of the Wolf pack. I think that my ancestry had something to do with it. Ishmael had a massive effect on him. Metisse, on the other hand, was a man of the world. He should have been more open-minded. And here he was, acting like a spoiled child who had to share his toys.

'You have to choose,' he declared once he'd regained his voice.

'I don't,' I answered calmly.

'You can't have both of us. It's him or me.' He attempted in vain to sound strong and to assert himself.

I turned towards him. 'Have you thought this through, Metisse?' I gave him the chance to back off. He didn't take it.

'Have you even contemplated the idea that if you force me to choose, I might not pick you?'

He hadn't.

The shock on his face was complete. His eyes opened to their fullest. His mouth gaped in shock. 'What will happen to you? How will you fight the bond we have?' My words registered.

'You don't have to choose.' Gabriel joined the conversation. 'The imprint will not let you choose him. You and I are soulmates. We are bonded. We need each other more than air itself. Without each other we will die.'

'Ahh,' I answered. 'That's where you're wrong. I have all the pros of the Wolf and none of the cons. You are bound by imprinting, I am not. I can take it or leave it. Whatever I want. You cannot refuse what your body and your Wolf demands of you. You physically and mentally need to be with me.'

I turned to Metisse.

'The same applies to you. You know I am the one your Sabre cries out for. You will wither and die without me.'

Now they were both in the same catch-22. Forcing me to make a choice would hurt at least one of them—probably both—much more than it would me. They would physically wither and die. I would live on. With whomever I chose—or neither of them, if they kept pushing me.

Both looked to their elders for support. Gabriel to Ash and Metisse to his mother. But they could not help. No one could. This was up to them. And me. Actually, mostly me.

I waited for them to come to a decision.

'This can never work.' Gabriel broke the impasse. 'You can come into the pack, it's where you belong. But not him. There is no way that this cat will be part of our pack.'

'Hell no. And the same applies for you,' Metisse countered loudly. 'You come into our clan and we'll kill you.' They proceeded to threaten each other. Shouting insults and mockery. Almost coming to blows.

I was flabbergasted. How dumb were they? Why couldn't they see further than their stupid testosterone fuelled macho bullshit?

'You really don't get it? Do you?' I shouted above the din.

They stopped their posturing just enough to look at me. Surprise shone in both their faces. Could be because I had the audacity to interrupt them. Might just as well be the fur that sprouted on my bare arms and the depth of the half-roar that accompanied my words.

'You are so thick.' Again, I looked at them both to make sure that they knew that they were both included in the comment. I measured my words carefully for maximum impact.

I turned to Gabriel, fire gleaming from my eyes. 'I will never be part of your pack.' He flinched. The repercussions of a failed imprint clear to everyone.

I turned to Metisse, ready to push that arrogant smirk off his face. 'And I'll never be part of your clan either.' The shock registered as he turned pale, his eyes open wide and his lips stuck in an unspoken exclamation.

That was when I pushed home the new order.

'You will both be part of mine.'

Chapter Fifty-Two

Charmaine and Ash were all smiles.

That was more than I could say for my two lovers. They were in deep shock.

Metisse's mother moved towards me and took my hands again as she looked me in the eye. Was that pride I saw?

'It's time,' she said enthusiastically. 'Let's bring down the Council.'

Chapter Fifty-Three

'When are you finally going to kill them?' Alex could barely keep the edge out of his voice. Red blotches started to cover his face, a sure sign of anger. Not that I was impressed. Just amused really.

'I'm not,' I said nonchalantly. My gaze never left the book I was leafing through. From the corner of my eye, I saw his brow crunch up in puzzlement.

'What do you mean?' he stammered, a slight tremor in his voice.

I looked up and locked eyes with him. As usual, he tried to avoid my gaze, but this time I wouldn't let him.

'I'm not going to kill them,' I said slowly, letting every word sink in. And that they did. The red colour in his face slowly faded until he became very pale. His eyes jittered from my face to his hands, and back again.

'Of course, you are,' he tried. 'That's your mission.'

'No,' I answered. 'My mission was to stop the war between the Werewolves and the Sabres.'

'But.' He looked decidedly sick. Paler than a live person should be. 'But that's not what she meant.'

'I know.' That didn't make him feel any better. My lips curled up into a smile. There was no mirth there. This was finally my pay back.

'But Cantix will not be pleased,' he tried again. His voice became progressively softer, harder to hear. Every word brought home the impact of my decision on his future, or lack thereof. He was grasping straws now in desperation.

'It's not really Cantix you're afraid of, is it?'

I put the book down on the table and slowly moved around the side to come close to him. He stepped back, his eyes opening to their fullest. He raised his arms in front of his chest in an attempt to shield off what he thought would happen. A bit premature. He was no use to me dead. He was a spy, and now he could pass my message on to his bosses. That they would probably kill him, was no skin off my back.

'What do you think Aquanaris will do to you Alex, when you tell her the plan has backfired?'

He stepped back, I matched his movement and kept the distance between us agonisingly small. 'You are probably right,' I added. The fear for his fate was clearly visible in his face. 'I'll give you a break though.' I was very close to him now. His back came up against the post and stopped his retreat. 'I'll give you the information Aquanaris really sent you to get.' He looked surprised.

'What…uh…what information?'

I laughed. He swallowed heavily. He took short breaths, trying in vain to melt into the barrier behind him.

'What I really am,' I said.

He stopped breathing.

'She wants to know what I really am. That's why you discreetly kept trying to touch me. I know she gave you some of her power to feel a subject.' I didn't actually know, but the faint involuntary nod confirmed my suspicion.

I lifted my arms up in an open gesture. 'Come on,' I added. 'Touch me. Find out what she so desperately needs to know.'

He looked puzzled. Cocked his head to one side. Was I really allowing him to feel my origin?

Slowly, very slowly, Alex moved his right hand towards my face. The head is by far the best place to read someone. Hands will work, but the face is best. He pulled back, cautious. When I didn't move, he tried again. How long did this guy need? My patience was wearing thin. But, then again, I was enjoying the moment.

I took his hand in mine and placed it on my cheek. He tried to pull back, but I held him firm. His eyes almost bulged out of his head as he read what was now obvious. He started to shake uncontrollably. His bladder emptied in panic; the acrid smell assailed my sensitive nose. His skin turned sickly white. Even paler than before.

He knew.

Alex's legs shuddered as I let go of his hand and he collapsed onto the floor. Soft keening noises rose from his mouth. He bent his neck forward and covered his head with his arms. All in an attempt to block out what he'd just learned.

I was the one in the prophecy; the Lamaq. I was the one who would bring down the Council.

And he was the messenger.

vinci-books.com/prophecy

The Council wants me dead, but an army has risen behind me.

Four months ago, I was an assassin driven by my obsession for revenge. No ties or complications bound me, my only desire being to right the wrongs of the past. Then, I learned I was the centre of an age-old prophecy, foretold to be the salvation of the world.

Can I convince my mates and followers to put their differences aside and stand together in the battle to come?

Turn the page for a free preview…

The Prophecy: Prologue

Life seemed so straightforward a few months ago.

Kill two targets and get out.

Then return to my real reason for living; find out who's responsible for my mother's death. I wanted to terminate him—or her—in a very painful, prolonged and terrible manner.

Whether I lived or died after achieving my revenge was completely irrelevant to me.

And now?

Now, I'm the centre of what is turning out to be a world changing prophecy.

How the fuck did that happen?

And another thing; I'm involved in not one but two romances. And to make things worse, both of my lovers have a legitimate claim to me as their soulmate.

The ideal solution seemed to be a threesome. It could work you know. If they weren't so different. And both so very, very possessive. Oh yeah, small detail. One is of the feline persuasion; a Sabre-tooth, and the other is a Werewolf.

Cat versus dog. The age-old adversity.

Times about a thousand.

It's a wonder I'm still sane.

That I am is solely the accomplishment of one man: Ash. The Blackfoot Shaman.

If he is a man that is.

He could be anything.

…Probably is.

The Prophecy: Chapter One

No one said it would be easy, but this is ridiculous.

My two beaus act like prepubescent adolescents.

Both of them.

Add the whole cat and dog thing to the equation and you get an idea why I'm going crazy.

"Why choose?" That's what Ash said. Yeah, why choose?

Well, I have more than enough reasons now why I should have chosen.

They have to share me. We established that months ago. Neither of them was particularly enthusiastic about the idea, but you'd think that they could at least be civil about it all. Pretend to be adults.

Metisse is the worst.

He's a lot younger than Gabriel, but I expected more from him because of his worldly and privileged upbringing. He was brought up in a society where strong females are the norm. His mother was—and really still is—the leader of one of the most influential Sabre clans in the world. He should know better.

Gabriel started off okay, but his patience with his rival was short to start with, and Metisse's childish behaviour pushed him to return in kind. Now he's just as bad.

Single life never looked as attractive as it does now. This was definitely not what I envisioned my life to become.

Four months ago, I was alone and my only goal in life was revenge for my mother's death. Romance was the last thing on my mind.

Ever since my mother was taken from me by the Council, my only drive has been to find the miscreants responsible for her death.

I knew she was dead.

There wasn't a body, but there was so much blood she could never have survived. The bastards didn't even leave me her corpse to grieve.

I was alone. Twelve years old and on the run from a mighty organisation that wanted me dead. I had no idea why, only that it was because of who I was. What I was.

I'm half Sabre and half Werewolf. A hybrid. The only one apparently.

My mother was the queen of a Sabre clan, my father the alpha of a Werewolf pack; traditionally sworn enemies.

Against all odds, they fell in love. Then they had me and all hell broke loose. The Council wanted me because of an old prophecy. I am apparently the Lamaq; a woman of two worlds, destined to overthrow their tyranny. Cantix and his sidekick Aquanaris would be out of a job, and hopefully minus their heads.

They ruled the paranormal world together. Not officially, no, that was the Council. But the members of the so-called ruling committee couldn't even fart without approval from Cantix.

The seer—Aquanaris—was feared throughout the entire world. She could see what others tried to hide. Saw rebellion before it even started.

Except with me.

She never saw through my disguise. Never knew the one person they hunted most was in their inner circle, closing in on them with every assassination they tasked me to perform. Cantix trusted me and I suspect he enjoyed my bad-ass petulant ways. I suppose I amused him.

I don't think Aquanaris ever completely fell for it, not really. She knew there was something about me. I would have loved to see their faces when they heard the news; their top assassin was the Lamaq. The chosen one. The woman from the prophecy. The one they hunted.

And now, here I was, trying to gather an army to combat the Council. I have to convince people—who hate each other with a vengeance—to work together against their real enemy. They have to put their petty differences aside and go for the real deal.

Sounds easy, right?

Walk in the park.

Wrong.

I was way out of my depth here. Up shit creek without a boat, never mind a paddle.

Thank goodness for Ash.

Ash—or Askuwheteau, if you want a tongue twister—is the Shaman of the Blackfoot tribe, he is also the unofficial leader of the Wolves, though he will always contradict that. He's been around for God knows how long. Hundreds, maybe thousands of years. I don't even know what he is exactly. He's not a Werewolf, but he is revered amongst them.

He's an enigma.

And he's my best friend.

Ash helped me find my way in the life-changing madness I found myself in. Convince me there was structure to this, reason. Well, I can't find it. So, I just took his word for it.

He grounded me.

Not that he told me things outright. Oh no. He helped me find out for myself. He guided me without pushing me in a direction. He stood beside me.

My big friend was—and is—my rock.

In a different way than my two beaus, thank God for that. Another one would have been way too many. No, he actually helped me find my way and supported me.

Literally sometimes.

And then there's Charmaine. The de-facto leader of the Sabres. I know, Metisse was the official leader, but even he referred to his mother. She's the anchor of the clan. She's the most natural chieftain I have ever seen.

Charmaine's my mother-in-law, Metisse's mother, but she's also my confidant. My mentor even. She's such a strong woman; I look up to her no end.

There was one very unsettling thing about her though. She knew my mother. And every now and then I felt she knew so much more than she was telling me. About the prophecy, my family and mostly; about me.

My beau's.

Metisse the haughty arrogant Sabre, rich and powerful. And Gabriel, his complete antithesis. A biker. A Werewolf. Poor in monetary terms, but rich in family and the loyalty of his pack.

They're each other's opposites. Rich versus poor. Status versus outcast. Cat versus dog.

They had to share me. I recognised them both as my soulmates. They were bonded to me and I to them. This strange love triangle's an anomaly. Wolves and Sabres don't mingle. They hate each other. Always have. But here they had to live together. Quite the challenge.

There were benefits—mostly for me—but it wasn't smooth sailing. As I said earlier; they drove me mad. Both acted like spoiled teenagers.

I didn't have time for all this crap.

Not then, now, not ever.

We were all pawns in the game destiny played with us; the prophecy. Seems that a woman of two worlds—me— would overthrow the Council.

The prophecy very conveniently didn't explain how I was supposed to do that monumental feat.

I'm not a strategist. I'm an assassin. A loner. I had no idea how to dethrone the Council.

But I did know I wanted to.

I had to.

For my parents.

…For me.

Okay, you're up to speed.

If you now think that this is all too ridiculous to be true.

…welcome to my world.

The Prophecy: Chapter Two

'I'm not a leader.'

I tried to make the statement as compelling and clear as possible. I knew I wasn't and never would be leader material. It was time the rest acknowledged that as well.

Yeah. Right.

Like that was going to happen. They all looked to me for guidance. Me!

'You are now.' Ash answered with a big smile. Sometimes, just sometimes, I wanted to knock that smile off his face. Good thing I couldn't reach it. The big man loved to bait me. And I presumed he was doing just that.

'Seriously, Trish,' he continued. All earnest again. 'You are the chosen one. The one person everyone refers to. You must lead us.'

"Chosen One." God, how I hated that phrase.

'How the hell am I supposed to do that?' I paced the room. I didn't want this, but no one was asking.

'I don't know how the fuck to lead people in battle. I'm an assassin, for fuck's sake. I'm not good with groups.'

There were a lot of "fucks" in my vocabulary as of late. What, with this crap and my two lovers at each other's throats all the time, it's inevitable.

'I work alone.'

'Not any more you don't.' There was no hesitation. No emotion. He was clearly stating the obvious. All the people who joined us in the past month were here because of me. Me, and a stupid prophecy they all wanted to believe in.

Yeah, well. I still want to believe in Father Christmas. Doesn't mean he's real. Wanting is not enough.

'Ash.' I tried a different tactic. 'I don't know what to do. I'm not leader material. I don't know how to motivate people, how to get them to fight for me, for a cause. That's not me. I'll get everyone killed.'

Nope, didn't work either. He just sat there and watched me get it out of my system. The man had patience. I didn't. Probably never will.

I stood still and ran my hand through my long red hair. I wanted to pull it out. Scream. Anything that would let out the tension that ate at me.

It wouldn't help. I knew that. Somewhere deep down inside a voice kept repeating this was my life now. I was here for a reason. They followed me for a reason.

Yeah, well, fucked if I knew what it was.

I sighed, squeezed my brow with my hand and closed my eyes. Let it all go away, please.

Nope, still there when I opened them. Only now Ash stood in front of me and looked down at my pathetic excuse for leadership.

He took my hands in his, dwarfing them. I felt like a small child every time he did that. He was so big, and I felt so tiny. Small, but safe.

'You need to have more faith in yourself, Trish.' He

made it all sound so easy. Okay, I'll do that. Sure. That simple, huh?

I swear the man could read my mind, he started to laugh. I looked up from under my eyebrows and bit my lip. My feline claws descended a bit and almost punctured the skin of his hands. He stayed put, the smile still plastered to his lips. I relaxed. The claws became regular nails again and I returned the smile.

'I suppose you find that funny?' I asked in mock anger.

He nodded. 'And so should you. Trish, there is no escaping who you are, or what you are. You might just as well embrace it. It will make life a lot easier for you.'

'And for me,' I heard from behind me. I let go of Ash's hands and turned to face an equally grinning Gabriel. I hadn't even heard him slink into the room. He liked to do that; surprise me.

'Is life with me that bad?' I asked him surprised.

'You have no idea.' The smile on his face was ear to ear. I tried to look angry but lost the fight quickly. I looked to Ash for support, he just shrugged and backed away laughing.

'Oh no, I'm not intervening in this one.'

'Wimp.' I muttered under my breath, just loud enough for him to hear.

'Oh, so your life is hard, is it?' I advanced on my lover who put his hands up in mock fear as he took a step back. At the last moment he reached out and took me in a massive bear hug, laughing all the time.

'You have no idea,' he repeated.

I tickled him. My fingers deep in his left side, just under the ribs. He's extremely ticklish and I know exactly the right spots. He doubled up, trying in vain to escape my hands. No way; when I have a hold, I don't let go.

Oh no. He changed tactics and went on the offence, finding my ticklish parts. Now I had to defend myself from someone who was a lot taller and heavier than me. Gabriel was spurred on by my struggles and Ash's laughter. It was silly. Childish, but we all needed this.

Suddenly Gabe stopped and stood up straight. Confused, I looked up at his face and then turned to follow his gaze. Metisse stood in the doorway, his face red and flushed; with jealousy probably. He hated to see me with Gabriel. It sparked off many arguments Between my beau's, and also between Metisse and myself.

Gabriel let go of me, his hands dropped to his sides as he watched what his love-opponent would do next.

I could see the struggle in Metisse's body language. He was tense, his clenched fists stiff by his sides. His thin lips were pulled into a straight line, echoing the anger I saw in his bright ochre eyes.

What would he do? Turn and leave? It wouldn't be the first time. He had a habit of avoiding situations like this. There would be days when I wouldn't see him at all. Other times he would be protectively, almost territorially present. He wouldn't leave my side. It was one extreme or the other. Absent or oppressively close.

He made up his mind and walked stiffly over to me where he stopped much too close. I felt Gabriel stand his ground. He didn't step back. Again, the ochre eyes flared as Metisse glared at Gabe over my head.

Okay, this was starting to piss me off again. Any good feelings I had were replaced by irritation. Thanks, Metisse. I thought.

He kissed me on the lips, making a point. Yeah, to Gabe, not to me. God, these two were getting on my nerves with their petty macho bullshit. They both stood so close to me I felt boxed in.

I had no time for this crap. With a shrug I sidestepped away from both of them. If they wanted to pose, then they could do it without me. Fuck that.

I heard murmurs behind me, they were at it again, shooting insults at each other. Did they honestly think I didn't hear them? I'm not deaf, you know.

I turned around, mad as hell. 'Can it.' The tone of my voice was hard enough to stop them mid-sentence. 'Grow up, both of you.'

They each looked at me with surprised faces and a "he started it" on the tip of their tongue. 'Don't,' I warned them. I must have looked serious, because they both shut up and looked embarrassed, as well they should. They were acting like children arguing over a toy. I'm not a toy and I will not accept this kind of behaviour.

Okay, I know this threesome was my idea. But if they didn't agree, then they should have said so.

It's not really that simple, I know.

They are both bound to me. They can't really refuse.

Not without endangering their own existence.

Grab your copy...
vinci-books.com/prophecy

About the Author

USA Today bestselling author Monique Singleton writes compelling stories that mix fantasy and science fiction with realistic psychological suspense and unique insights into the mind of the main characters.

As the daughter of a British soldier and his Dutch wife, Monique was born in an English military hospital in Germany. The family toured the world where she was exposed to different cultures in many countries. Finally settling down in the Netherlands she pursued a career in Art and later in consultancy.

In 2017, Monique started to put the scenes she had running around in her head, down to paper. Scenes led to a story, the story to a book, and the first book to a series. The rest is, as we say, is history. She has now penned many books in multiple series.

In addition to her writing, Monique still holds down a full-time job as a business consultant. She lives in a beautiful old farmhouse in the south of Holland with her two sloppy monster dogs, a horse, and two cats.

The cats are the boss.